Nun's Castle

Also by Jennie Melville

A NEW KIND OF KILLER
HUNTER IN THE SHADOWS
IRONWOOD

Nun's Castle

JENNIE MELVILLE

David McKay Company, Inc.
New York

Nun's Castle

COPYRIGHT © 1973 BY JENNIE MELVILLE

All rights reserved, including the right to reproduce this book, or parts thereof, in any form, except for the inclusion of brief quotations in a review.

LIBRARY OF CONGRESS CATALOG CARD NUMBER: 73-84060

MANUFACTURED IN THE UNITED STATES OF AMERICA

ISBN: 0-679-50411-7

Nun's Castle

Chapter One

The tower at Nun's Castle still stands, staring out doggedly on the countryside it once dominated, a ruin, all that is left of a proud castle. Several times razed to the ground, as often rebuilt, finally betrayed, it still retains something of its original menace. Yet even its proper name is gone, and it is called now, in country parlance, after the ruins of the nunnery it once looked down upon. I am not fond of it; it has harmed me too much. Yet, strangely, it has the power to bring the past to life.

I once attended a coronation and a christening all on the same day. Not many people have done that, I should think—not in the twentieth century. I believe I was more surprised to be at the christening than the coronation, but they were both stage-managed beautifully and I enjoyed every minute of them. My role in both ceremonies was not elevated. It would have been strange if it had been. I was there in the old abbey chapel entirely as an expert to oversee the details. I am a historian, a graduate of an ancient university, and a student of social custom through the centuries. At that time I was writing a book on the running of a royal household in the thirteenth century, working mainly in the British Museum. I know a good deal about coronations:—in an academic way, of course. I don't know so much about christenings. There is very little detail about christenings in the records, but I suppose they don't vary much up and down the centuries. You have the baby and the priest and a name and that's it; the ritual can hardly alter very much. In this case, they did it, as I have said, beautifully. They even had a real baby. I was a little surprised at that. It wasn't a very young baby; you could hardly expect it to be. Most mothers would find it hard to see their child lifted up by a man in flowing gown and mock ermine and handed over to another wearing an archbishop's cope and then freely doused with water and oil as was the medieval custom. I was only astonished to see they had got an infant at all. It was a good healthy blue-eyed boy with red hair and about nine months old, I should judge. He didn't cry, but stared at us with a knowledgeable air. He got very angry toward the end of the rather protracted business, however, and I think he kicked the Archbishop. I saw him wince. The Archbishop looked tired, but then he had had a principal part to play in both ceremonies, and moreover I happened to know he had been out hunting all the previous day.

    I remember going to the chapel window, the one in the south aisle, and staring out. The glass was ancient, but the great window still stood sturdily and you got a fine view down the valley. Everything was tinted the fine soft green of early summer. The slope of the hill opposite was covered with old deciduous trees, descendants of the medieval forest that had stood there, a hunting place for princes. Time had thinned out the forest, but had not entirely destroyed it. I could not see the water but I knew a small river wound its way through the country at the foot of the hill. It was a well-watered landscape, as the rich vegetation indicated, with many streams and deep pools and muddy paths: a luxuriant, treacherous world to the hunted animal, not really affording the refuge it appeared to promise. My eyesight is keen, and as I looked through the window I fancied I could perceive the very shape of the oak leaves, and the glossy oval beech leaves. I saw a little cat creeping across the hill, carrying something white in its mouth, a bird, I supposed. As it came closer I saw it was only a piece of paper. I watched the gray figure disappear under a tree, just a harmless little cat that hunted paper balls.

My view was straight across the valley of the river Wye. On either side of me stretched the Welsh Marches, those rich border lands assigned by medieval kings to protect the midlands of England from invasion by the turbulent Welsh. To the north were the Shropshire castles of Clun, Hopton and Stokesay, the great keep of Chester; to the south lay the castles of Edward I. Nun's Castle, where I stood, was almost in the middle. Here I was in a countryside of small farms, old centers of habitation whose history probably went back to the Iron Age. Nun's Castle was more than a farm. It had a handsome great house built in the late eighteenth century; it had, in addition, the chapel, and across the valley, clinging to a hilltop, it had the ruins of the castle itself. Now the nuns were long gone and the castle, except for the tower (called Catt's Tower locally), was a romantic ruin, Nun's

Castle no more than the name of a scattered group of dwellings. But it remained a strange place, with curious hints of violence and murder long ago. In the history of this land there have been many heroes, some real, some creatures of myth. One of the most enigmatic (except for the great King Arthur himself) was Llywellyn, the last native-born Prince of Wales. He was the son of Owain, a fat, red-headed man who killed himself trying to escape from the Tower of London by means of a rope too fragile to bear his weight. Llywellyn fell in love with and married a girl much younger than himself, the King's niece into the bargain. She was the child of an even more romantic match, the elopement of the King's sister with Simon de Montfort, rebel against the King. This ill-starred marriage brought the Prince into a situation where he had to face the anger (hidden, but real) of the King and the treachery of his own supporters. He was lured to his death and murdered, possibly by his own cousins, not far from Nun's Castle, and near the river. The last night of his life he spent in Catt's Tower. His wife died in childbirth and the infant Princess, so dangerously close to the English throne, was put into a nunnery by her royal uncle (a fate often reserved for inconvenient heiresses), where it was hoped she would die unwed. So she did, history says, but there is a legend that she escaped and married a local landowner. Joe, Lynnet, David and I were brought up on this story. We were great storytellers as children, full of tales like Ednyfed's Harp and the Bride, and of Arthur and his sleeping warriors. Who can tell what is true, what untrue? So many things lie buried in the labyrinth of history.

Behind me I could hear a melodious voice intoning, then the music of a flute, then silence. I leaned my head against the cool stone wall—it had begun to ache a little. Suddenly amazement at what we were doing swept over me. We were all mad, all of us.

I straightened myself and turned briskly. My neighbor, a stout matron dressed in red and wearing a Burgundian head-dress, mopped her forehead. The sleeves of her long gown were lined with miniver and from these luxurious sleeves of plum-colored velvet stretched two thick wrists and stained hands. I knew she was an ardent gardener.

I swung my gaze back to the scene in front of me, bemused and entranced. We were a small congregation but very colorful. Red velvet, deep like a damson, Damascene glinting with gold thread, furred hoods, rich surcoats lined with beaver. Well, it could be cold in there; the spring winds blew coldly, and the flagged floor could gleam with dampness. However, the day had turned warm and many of the distinguished guests were sweating. Earl de Bohun was quietly dabbing his face with a fine linen square. Across the aisle the High Constable of Builth Castle was enduring stoically, his noble profile like alabaster. His wife, however, looked flushed.

The Archbishop finished, gave a sort of hitch to his robes and limped down the aisle toward the door leading to fresh air and sunlight.

According to strict protocol the Prince should have gone first, but perhaps we were not playing that game any more. I followed very slowly, so that I was last out of the chapel, and when I got out on to the smooth green turf it was dotted with chattering groups. I could see the Prince and the Archbishop talking to each other and Lady Dorothy wagging a finger. The baby seemed to have disappeared. I could sense a slight air of discouragement in nearly everyone present. I looked at them with sympathy. I had done my job. They were just beginning.

The whole conception was that of Lady Dorothy, the owner of the Dower House, but I thought I had attended to the technical details very well. One hundred years ago, one of her great-great grandfathers had organized a tournament at Nun's Castle. There are many accounts and some striking early photographs of the mid-nineteenth-century nobility and gentry assembled in armor (expensively made by the local blacksmith), complete with pages and horses. The ladies were placed in gaily bedecked stands to watch their knights joust. In the stiff old photographs everyone is carefully posed and ardently pre-Raphaelite. Icily elegant, splendidly null, there they stand, staring into the camera's empty eye. It was this forebear's wife, aided by her friend Ruskin, who had restored the chapel. With her own hands she had recreated a fine fourteenth-century wall painting of the royal patrons of the abbey. Lady Dorothy herself had inherited her great-great grandmother's tastes and skills. Recently she had retouched the now fading Plantagenet portraits. She had endowed them all with romantic and handsome features, very unlike what the original donors must have possessed. There was, in any case, some mystery, as no one knew who they were. The chapel had, at some time in the early fourteenth century, been richly endowed, and nothing more was known for sure. One personage in the group seemed to wear a crown, and on the hem of her skirt were written the words "Our Lady, the Princess." I suspected Lady Dorothy of having painted these words, but perhaps I misjudged her. She had certainly restored to the Princess a noble and striking face and a mass of tawny hair.

And now she had conceived the idea of staging afresh that forgotten Victorian tournament, as a performance for charity, to be enacted by her neighbors, wearing the original clothes, most of which were still packed away in mothballs in trunks and wardrobes in various homes. But she had gotten carried away and elaborated her ideas into a coronation, on which she asked for my advice, and a christening as well. About the christening she was reticent, even secretive, and kept it from me as long as she could, which annoyed me at the time because I thought it showed a feeling she had overreached herself. But I was wrong; it was not her motive.

She was full of enthusiasm and had explained how much it would do for the neighborhood, bringing in tourists by the hundreds. It would look marvelous on videotape and the local television company had contributed financially. I wasn't sure about it all, but I helped all the same—safely from a distance in London. I'm a good letter writer.

I thought, at that moment, that I could turn round and walk away and leave them all to it; that I could cease to be what I was to them then, a relative stranger, although one who knew a great deal about them and their lives in a detached kind of way, and go back to being what I preferred to be, just someone who had built up a life of her own. I was the local girl who had made good. Now I could return to my own life and enjoy it.

I knew every inch of this piece of countryside, as it was now and as it had been once. I was standing on grass, but long ago it had been a paved courtyard. To the right of where I was standing had been a cloister. Beyond this had stretched the complex of the abbey's domestic buildings, quite small but probably very beautiful.

A hand touched my arm and a familiar voice said: "Selina."

I smiled to myself, and turning to Ted Lestrange, who had appeared at my side, I said: "There was a nunnery here once. It housed twenty-three nuns."

"You wouldn't have enjoyed living in a nunnery. You'd have been miserable."

"It wasn't a bad life. You mustn't think of it as a hard one. Those twenty-three nuns were sitting on the top of a pyramid of lay workers, servants and laborers; they were leisured ladies. I doubt if they got their hands dirty."

"Well, good for them. Speaking as an honest working farmer, I wouldn't mind a bit of that."

I smiled at him. It's funny looking at a man and knowing one could say to him: your grandfather married his own second cousin, a girl called Eleanor, who brought the Fitzwarin blood into the family, a very interesting legacy which may account for a lot about you; you remain on your own soil, and the men who work for you have probably as deep roots as you have. The population pattern has been remarkably stable. There was an extraordinary continuity and persistence in this countryside. The unusual blood groups of some of the population matched the blood groups of people still living in the Iberian peninsula. This suggested, to historians, at any rate, that the possessors of such rare blood types in my native land were descended from Bronze Age immigrants always thought to have come from the coast of Spain. The same blood groups have been traced in the men in the Iron Age grave, in the medieval tombs and in men like you, my friend. Your great grandfather was said physically to resemble his remote ancestor the Lord Clifford of Edwarden, who was in turn said to be like a remoter ancestor of pure Celtic stock. That's where you get your black, black hair. You and your family have farmed here for generations. At one time you were an important baronial family, now you're just farmers, but you're still here, walking the soil you own.

I could say all this to him. I could also say: You are reputed to descend from a bastard of Roger Mortimer, Lord of Chirk. If so, you are certainly related to the men who murdered Edward II in Berkeley Castle, and sometimes, I could say, you look as though you could be up to that sort of thing yourself.

I could say it and still find him an attractive man. I'm afraid he knew it, too. I have a natural poker face and I was playing it cool, but it shows in other ways. I would have been glad to know the attraction was mutual, nothing too serious, you know, but felt by both parties. Unluckily for me (apart from his ancestry, land-owning and hereditary blood grouping) he was an enigma. I *never* knew what he really thought. Without being in the least good-looking, Ted was a very attractive person. Perhaps because everything about him from his old Burberry to his motor car, without being in the least contrived or fussy, looked as if they were made for him and him only and could never have been used by any other person. I don't know where he bought his clothes, or even if he did buy many, for they never looked new, but they always looked as right on him as the bark on a tree. Ted was a very *natural* person.

I walked away from him down the soft grass. I was planning to leave that afternoon. I was going to get into my motor car and spin off down the motorway and home.

The job I had come for was done.

I believed now that my cousin Lynnet had certainly run

away, did not wish to come back, and had cut all links between herself and this rich valley. I had read the letter she had written to say so. As a historian I felt it was a piece of evidence I was bound to accept, provided it satisfied various tests of authenticity, of course. This letter was authentic. The sentences sprawled across the page, there were no commas, and she couldn't spell "desperate"; yes, Lynnet had written it.

Lady Dorothy saw me standing in the sunlight and came over. She was my employer. Or rather, she had been until eleven-thirty that morning, when she had given me a check and a smile and a gentle shake of the hand and my job was done. As I had accepted her hand I had felt just as I used to do years ago when I was a child and she used to ride over in her rattling little car and bring Christmas or birthday presents for me and Lynnet. I felt glad to see her, delighted at what she was offering, and deeply irritated, within about three minutes.

"Off now, then, are you, Selina?" she said, with her usual maddening way of seeming to know what you were about to do better than you did yourself. It had the usual perverse effect on me.

"I did mean to, but I might stay a bit longer."

"You should know your own mind, dear, and not let other people influence you." She looked across at Edward Lestrange and I knew exactly what she meant. "You always did let people influence you as a little girl."

I looked at her reproachfully.

"Oh no, not weak, dear, just much too kind-hearted."

"I'm not being kind-hearted to Edward Lestrange, the brute."

"No, indeed, dear, I shouldn't advise it. He is well able to look after himself." Between Lady Dorothy and Ted Lestrange, two strong-minded, self-assertive characters, there were frequent brushes. "I had to threaten to sue him over the pasture rights due to me in the hill farm at Over Hill."

I could have told Lady Dorothy of an ancestress of hers called Hawissa who had been engaged in constant litigation with her neighbor in the fourteenth century. I had learnt a good deal about the medieval law of property from the doings of Hawissa, but sometimes, especially lately, she and Lady Dorothy got muddled in my mind. As for example, now, when I had to stop myself from pointing out that she'd tried this in 1358 and had had to give way.

"What did he do?" I asked.

"Threatened me back," she said with relish. "My goodness, you have to keep your eye on the ball with that one."

She walked with me to the car, carrying her long robes with dignity and assurance. I was the only one of those present who was wearing contemporary dress. Lady Dorothy had protested but I was adamant. "I'm here as a technical adviser only," I had said. She had by no means abandoned the idea even now. "You'd look splendid dressed as a page," she said. "You've got the legs, nice and straight and slim. It's a mistake to think you want too much calf, you know," she said earnestly. "Especially if we're going to be televised, which makes everyone look fatter. I could dress you beautifully as the page of the Earl of March. You ought to do it; remember, you're a landowner here now. The Earl really needs another one; the one he had is frightened of horses, silly girl."

"I'm frightened of horses," I said.

"No, you're not—not frightened of anything." She looked at me cheerfully. "Wonderful spirit." I might have been a horse myself that she was praising. I did wonder sometimes if she distinguished sharply between her friends and the animals that surrounded her. She worked the lot of us as hard as she could. "If you're driving off you can take David home with you. His car's broken down again. I never knew a worse man with machinery than he is."

David Griffith was one of my oldest friends. Dorothy had a protective affection for him which she thought licensed her to be rude to him. He was never rude back and I admired him for this because I sometimes saw a glint in his eye which hinted at a temper kept under command.

"It's a poor old car," I said tolerantly. I always took David Griffith's side when he was criticized, although I was sometimes one of his harshest critics. I suppose he could have afforded a new car if he'd really wanted to, but on a budget as tight as I knew David's to be, if one thing comes in another must go out. I thought he'd drive the old car till it dropped beneath him. "He's changed," I said, watching his unmistakable figure move across the grass toward us. A gust of wind caught his cloak and it billowed out about him. He caught it gracefully.

"How many years is it since you last saw him?"

"Five years, nearly six."

"Ah," she said, shrugging. "He was a boy then; he's a man now."

"Yes." I looked at his face. "What's happened to him?"

"He's been losing money with his farm lately. Well, who hasn't? But he may have to sell the whole place."

"He'll be better off without it." I thought David Griffith's obsession with his ancient home and farm overdone. Even as a child he had been obsessed with it.

"They've had it for generations," protested Lady Dorothy. Her own family had known how to hang on to its possessions and even grab more. Which accounted for the fact that the great mansion at Nun's Castle was now her property, while all that remained to Joe and Lynnet, the descendants of the original owners, was the old castle tower, some adjoining ruins, and many barren acres on which not even the sheep prospered.

A hundred years ago our ancestors had drawn profits from the copper mined there, but this had long since been abandoned. There was nothing profitable to be done with the land as a consequence; we were the poorer now for having been the richer then. Our land extended uphill to the moors and downhill to the river, where it was fordable. A narrow stone bridge crossed the river farther downstream. It all formed a composed and beautiful landscape, which I loved.

People said you could tell that Joe and Lynnet and I were closely related by the way we looked, but I always thought you could tell the blood tie by our voices and the way we talked, the very words we used and the jokes we made. Whether we liked it or not these bore witness to our having been cousins who were brought up together. In spite of quarrels we never forgot our childhood and our common ancestry. It was "our" land and "our" ancestry even to me, the one who had fled.

"And then, that girl he was engaged to broke it off."

"No loss, I should think."

"Just because you've got a heart of stone toward men, my dear, doesn't mean everyone is the same." Then she saw she might have hurt me. "No offense, my dear, I'm the same myself."

Rubbish, I thought. She had found the male animal attractive and interesting and had done so since she was a bright-eyed little girl flirting with her father's groom. She had quite a history and well I knew it. Whereas I had come by my cool heart the hard way.

She patted my hand. "You were always too clever, Selina," she said wistfully. "It's been hard on you, yourself, my dear. I'm not sure you're quite fit yet, you must take care! I know how it's been with you and Joe and Lynnet. As we spin, so shall we weave." She sighed. "I blame your grandfather."

"I'll take David home," was all I said. This was no time to talk of family wars and politics.

I greeted David with a smile, I could just manage to do that, and led him toward the house. "My car's outside," I said. "Can you manage that robe, or shall I help you with it?"

"I can manage," he said briefly and strode beside me on the grass. The Prince's mantle became him well and he wore it more easily than most of the other actors. His was real old velvet and the ermine, although yellow with age, was genuine. His robe was one hundred and twenty years old. "The christening went well, didn't it?"

"I thought the baby would bite the Archbishop," I said. "Why did you have a christening? I thought it would end with the coronation of the Prince."

"Ah, it leads forward to the next generation, you see, it's symbolic."

"Well, Henry hated it." Henry was the Archbishop.

"Yes, he hates it all really, but he daren't offend Lady D. He does look superb, doesn't he?"

One of Henry's ancestors had been a nephew of a thirteenth-century Bishop of St. Asaph. Classifying anyone as a medieval episcopal nephew was well known to be a polite way of indicating a natural son, so that Henry had, under the blanket, got a claim to clerical blood. His blood had run a bit secular now, though, and with Henry it saw more of the hunting field than the church, but perhaps it always had.

"And where did the baby come from?" I asked politely.

"I think it belongs on one of the farms."

"A good little roarer, wasn't it?"

"It was hungry, I think." He sounded preoccupied. Across the grass I could see Ted Lestrange keeping a weather eye on us both. Trust him. We were walking slower and slower as we came closer to the river which ran through the valley. The water was low and easily forded on the chain of stepping stones. I stepped delicately and carefully all the same because this was how I had learnt to cross as a child.

On the other side, David stopped, and turned to face me. "Selina, can I talk to you?"

"Come to the Tower," I said. "I must pick up my traveling bag."

And I led him into the great hall of Catt's Tower, where it all—death, love and treachery—began.

Long ago when the scribes were writing down the

results of the great survey of England initiated by William the Conqueror, which was to be called the *Doomsday Book*, they dated their findings from the "day on which the good King Edward was alive and dead." For me the drama in which I eventually played the reluctant part must be said to have begun on the day a person I never knew, my great-grandfather, was alive and dead. He died very cheerfully, over a bottle of port, and he left his affairs in a terrible muddle. From then on we were, as a family, relatively poor and scratching around for the means to keep up what used to be called "position." Some income and valuable jewelry, gradually to be sold over the years, remained at his death, but compared with what should have been there it was nothing.

Everything stems from that, I think. All subsequent generations suffered, but my generation most of all. When I grew up there were three of us left. Myself, and my second cousins Joe and Lynnet. Joe was my great-grandfather's chief victim. He never had a chance. He was born clever, irritable and hopelessly crippled. He had great talents and could never make use of any of them. A complete countryman in many ways, he might have ridden to hounds and been a fine shot. (Lynnet was; and even I knew how to handle a gun.) He was also a man of affairs, active, he might have been a Member of Parliament. But in practice he could do nothing and Lynnet and I tried everything. We rode, climbed trees and swam in the river, avoiding with the cool nerve of the young the swirl of sucking waters we called The Devil's Sink. So the people he hated most of all in the world were his sister Lynnet and me. Lynnet was pretty and healthy, and I was clever. Between us we had everything he had, and vigorous life as well.

I didn't really wonder that Lynnet had run away.

When I first heard about it, I thought I'd have done it myself if I hadn't won a scholarship to a famous girls' boarding school and then another scholarship to Oxford and then another scholarship to Harvard to do research. I never really came home after I was twelve. I suppose you could say my brains bought me an out.

But Lynnet had only a pretty face and an affectionate heart, and so she had to run for it.

The story of her departure first came to me as hearsay in faraway Cambridge, Massachusetts, several months before I came home. I was told the general outlines by an American cousin of Lady Dorothy's who lived in Boston. Needless to say, among the other luxuries life provided for Lady Dorothy were kindred on the eastern seaboard of the United States, a second cousin married into a princely family in Rome and another who lived on a sugar plantation in Venezuela, surely the last stronghold of privilege left. Dorothy could never be at a loss; probably she had someone married "well" into the Kremlin if the truth were told. But she was generous, as always, with her riches, and gave introductions to her relations to all those she approved of, and I was one.

I was enjoying the early summer heat of a Boston suburb when I heard about Lynnet. Coming from a cold climate, I was enchanted to feel sweaty hot while all my American friends mopped and grumbled. I had my eyes closed and was pretending to drink iced tea. The only drawback to my visit was the cold tea. Being English, I was constantly offered tea, and since it was a very hot day the tea was iced, but, as any English person knows, tea can only be taken piping hot and rather strong. Cold tea is anathema.

Iced coffee, now, is different. I would have been delighted to drink iced coffee, but I was English and was offered tea.

"You must be worried about your cousin Lynnet," said my kind hostess. "Very distressing for you."

I opened my eyes. "What's that?"

"Lynnet, dear. Dorothy says she's very upset herself at the way the girl has taken herself off. Dorothy does take things to heart."

"Yes, she's very kind," I said mechanically. "But what's the story about Lynnet? I didn't know."

My hostess made a distressed noise. "My dear, I had no idea you didn't know."

I wasn't in close touch with my old home. I had deliberately set myself at a distance from it. I had met Lynnet for lunch in London before I flew to the States. Since then she had written a few of her hurried but loving little notes. Joe I hadn't been in touch with for quite some time.

"No, I didn't know," I said. The trouble was Lynnet couldn't really do anything. How would she support herself? She cooked delicious food, she sewed her own clothes, she rode a horse well, but she did it all diffidently, as if she doubted her own powers; and it was true that every so often disaster attended her, the dress was shapeless or she fell off her horse. She sang sweetly, but even here there was one fatal flaw: after a while she would lose the note and go flat or sharp, she could not hold a tone.

"She's simply run away. Left her home and gone."

Later I found out that Lady Dorothy had put things in her own way, and my kind hostess had softened the words. It may seem strange that such a local piece of news should cross the Atlantic, but I already knew that Dorothy and her cousin sent each other old-fashioned diary-style letters in which anything and everything figured. No doubt an account of my reception of the news would soon travel back across the Atlantic and had, perhaps, been asked for.

But I was well trained and kept a poker face. Inside, however, I was deeply distressed at what I heard. I didn't blame Lynnet for leaving Joe, I should have done it myself years before. I suppose you could say I had done so. Anyway, I took good care not to see him. But for Lynnet it was alarmingly out of character. She was the sort of person who smiled and endured.

"Where's she gone?"

"Dorothy doesn't know. I don't think anyone does. I remember meeting her. Such a pretty girl."

"But unlucky," I said, the words popping out like poisoned darts.

"An unlucky family." She shook her head. "My dear, when you've been around as long as I have, you know some people just *are* unlucky. It works itself out, though, in the end. Give it time."

I remember smiling and nodding. It seemed the only thing to do. I didn't know then that time was what Joe and Lynnet and I lacked.

I'll look for Lynnet when I go home, I promised myself, and get the truth out of her. I could always make Lynnet tell me things. It angered Joe that I had this power. He himself was like an old sorcerer sitting in the wings, who couldn't make his spells work. How funny that I should remember forming this thought. Since then I have wondered if Joe didn't, after all, put his spells on us and make them operate.

He might have told me about Lynnet, I thought; after all we did exchange a few letters. I was using our family letters and records going back to the seventeenth century (we had what amounted to an archive) for a piece of research, and this necessitated a letter every so often to Joe. By this means we kept in touch.

But I did not go home to Lynnet. Not then. Between me and the performance of my promise came a blank.

I was in a car, there was a curve in the road, one of those curves that look innocent. I was seated beside the driver. I remember the other car approaching, headlights blazing, and then I remember nothing. My memory of the weeks *before* my accident went too. Apparently this is a common, although tiresome, consequence of concussion. Sometimes I found myself recalling odd, isolated incidents. I remember shopping in New York and looking in the window of a smart store, Bonwit Teller's perhaps, and seeing a display of nursery furniture, including an elegant Moses basket of natural straw lined with soft cotton printed with red lions. Or were they dandelions? My mind played a joking pun on me and wouldn't say. Perplexing.

I was in a hospital for several weeks. It was a long while before the spells of dizziness left me, but the doctors said I was lucky and would make a complete recovery in time. About the post-accident amnesia they said nothing. Perhaps it didn't seem important to them.

As soon as I was better, except for a headache or two and an occasional nasty dream, I went back home to England. Arrangements were made for me to see a suitable specialist in London to check up on my recovery.

I hadn't forgotten Lynnet. The first move was obvious, but I put it off as long as I could. Then, wearing my bravest face, I went down to see Joe.

He refused to see me.

There was no question of pushing past the door and getting in. He had a daily woman who was also a nurse and she looked twice as strong as I, even if I'd wanted to fight. And have I said that Joe did not answer telephone calls? He didn't.

So that left Lady Dorothy, and I tried her. She was delighted to see me, warm and welcoming, knew as much about my accident as I did myself, and had obviously been expecting me to call.

"It's about Lynnet. I've tried to speak to Joe, but he won't see me."

"Heart's bad," she said briefly.

"It always was. Stone cold, hard and bad."

There was a pause. "I meant he's ill."

"He'll get better," I said. "People like Joe always do. It's people like Lynnet who get ground up into little bits."

She made a distressed noise. "My dear."

"Where is she?"

"I don't know, Selina. I wish I did. She took all her clothes, packed all her little treasures. Even the tiny furniture from the doll's house. That's very funny, you know."

"It means she's gone for good." The doll's house furniture and china was a hundred and fifty years old and valuable. In our grandmother's will Joe had been left Catt's Tower and its adjoining ruins; the whole estate was known as Nun's Castle. Lynnet and I had been left various chattels.

"I'm sorry to be no help," said Lady Dorothy, sighing.

But she had given me a weapon to use on Joe. I went to the door of the Tower, and sent in a note which read briefly, "I understand Lynnet took the doll's house furniture with her when she left. You remember grandmother left it jointly between us? If you don't let me come and see you then I shall go to old Powys, the solicitor in Hereford, and have him start a search for her, to recover my property."

He received me (you couldn't miss the royal word with Joe) lying on a sofa with a rug over his legs. We hadn't met for years, but I got no greeting. The same woman who had turned me away previously had this time admitted me, saying, as she did so, that she would be gone before I left but that "the girl who did the evening nursing" would be there. "You don't need to worry," she added dryly. "She's a good strong girl." I wasn't worrying. I was busy hating Joe.

He began: "It's no use asking me where Lynnet is. She's cleared out, the bitch, and that's that."

"I'd like to find her." Memories of Lynnet playing with her miniature toys while Joe looked on flooded back.

"She hasn't written to you, has she? She hasn't tried to see you? No. She wants out. Leave her."

"I don't like it."

"You ought to understand. You went first, didn't you?" His voice was hostile.

When I turned to go he picked up a glass of water that stood on a table by his side and deliberately threw it. It hit a pretty oak cabinet on the wall and made a dent in it. He could do it, too. His shoulders and arms were very strong.

Then he called me back. "Wait. Before you go I've got something to tell you. Since Lynnet went I've made a new will. I've left you the Tower."

"Thanks for nothing," I said. "I hope you live forever."

"But not straight out. I've made you and Lynnet joint heiresses." And he started to laugh.

"What's so funny about that?" I asked.

"It's one great big joke," he said, still laughing. "You'll find out."

For the first time, I wondered what he had done to Lynnet.

I went back to London, hating him. But Lady Dorothy was proved right and I was wrong. Joe died that night from what the doctor called "cardiac arrest." It meant his heart stopped.

In his will he had left Lynnet his invested capital and the ownership of several small farms which were leased to tenant farmers.

And I was left the Tower and the many many unprofitable acres amid which it stood. And Joe's debts. It was surprising that he'd managed to achieve so many, but he had.

Lynnet and I were co-heiresses. But Lynnet wasn't there, was she?

I came back to the present to find myself looking at David. "I don't know where Lynnet is," I said. "If that's what you were going to ask me."

He shook his head. "I was thinking of you really, and what you were going to do. Are you coming back here to live?"

"I don't intend to be a frequent visitor. I'd like to sell it. You could build a lot of small houses here."

"You can't do that." He was horrified.

"I can't do anything till Lynnet comes back," I said irritably. "You know the solicitors advertised and got nothing? That's why I'm here. I wanted to look around to see if I could find out anything about Lynnet."

"And did you?"

"I found a letter from Lynnet. It was addressed to me.

Stamped. Ready to post. Joe must have suppressed it. It was in the drawer of his bed table. I think he'd read it. It looked read. In it she said she was going away because she was desperate. So Joe didn't kill her after all."

"Did you think he had?"

I stood up. "For a little while, I did. Let's go, shall we, David?"

We went out, and I locked the great oak door behind me and left the Tower.

I had shut Joe and his ghost inside and Lynnet and I were on the outside now, and I hoped for ever.

David said shyly: "I want to show you something."

I was amused. "Something you've made?"

"No, oh no. It means taking a short walk. Will you do that? The field is not far from here."

"Is it a crop you are growing?"

He smiled. "Yes, a whole crop."

"I don't have much time."

"I think you'd like to see what I have done." He added coaxingly, "Only a few minutes' walk."

I went to please him. In the past I had often found myself doing things to please David: he had an engaging way with him.

We walked up the hill from Nun's Castle and then took a turn to the right down a short lane which ended in a padlocked gate.

I was curious. His own farm was some miles away. "I didn't know you had any land up here?"

"I rent it," he said absently.

He let me into a small, square, old-fashioned field, totally enclosed by a high hedge.

Inside, scattered in small groups, were some strange

animals. Slender, shaggy beasts, with thick coats, they had gentle, thoughtful faces.

"They're a sort of sheep," I said in wonder. "How leggy they are, and their coats seem more furry than woolly. What are they, David?"

"They're *sheep*," he said proudly. "What sheep were once. This is what sheep were like when men first began to herd them. Neolithic man knew sheep like this. Yes," he went on excitedly. "I heard that on a remote island off the Scottish coast was this herd that had been there untouched since the days of the Vikings and before. I went up there, got permission to buy some, and brought them here."

"They *do* look like the sheep in medieval drawings," I said.

David was triumphant. "I knew you'd be pleased, as an historian. Animals like this are a kind of national trust. They *ought* to be preserved."

"How did you hear about them?" I was fascinated by them. And by David too; he was full of surprises.

"Read in a magazine, went up and had a look."

I wondered at the cost: David was not rich, as I well knew. "It must have been expensive, David."

"Yes." He was brief. It struck me he might have got help from Lady Dorothy Wigmore. She might even have shown him the article about the sheep.

They seemed to know him, and gathered round to stare at him silently. They were sheeplike in that, at all events.

"I believe they are cleverer than modern sheep," I said, observing the narrow heads and bright eyes.

"Sheep aren't so stupid," said David defensively. "Some of my best friends are sheep."

He rarely made a joke, so I suppose, in a way, he meant what he said.

I drove myself back to London, leaving behind a David who had given me a quick fraternal kiss and hug. It meant nothing, I thought, but it had comforted and cheered me. I drove fast and happily, letting the radio sing out as I went.

Later that night when I went to put the milk bottles out, there was a little lost white kitten calling miserably at the door. I looked at it for a moment, not wanting to take it in, but something about its soft blue-eyed stare reminded me of Lynnet. I put my hand out and stroked its soft fur. It stopped mewing and arched its back and began to purr. There was no doing anything else with such an incurable optimist. I picked it up and carried it inside.

Chapter Two

The little cat was still with me the next morning. When I woke up she was sleeping peacefully on my pillow with her nose on her paws. I carried her gently back to the bed I had made for her in a box in my kitchen, and then put some coffee on.

Almost as soon as I'd finished my coffee, the telephone started to ring.

"Hello?"

"Is that Miss Selina Brewse? I have a call for you from Cardiff," said the operator blithely.

I waited. Then a brisk, masculine voice started. "Saxby, Moore and Bertey here. This is Mr. English speaking."

"Oh, yes," I said, wondering what was to come.

"I have a client who is interested in your property at Nun's Castle. He is prepared to make a good offer. I understand you are ready to sell."

"No, not ready at all."

"Oh, but I understood . . ."

"It is not in my power to sell at the moment," I said politely.

"Oh, but Miss Brewse . . ."

I was beginning to find Mr. English tiresome.

"No sale, Mr. English," I said, and put the receiver down.

I hadn't given up hope of finding Lynnet, by any means. I knew there were organizations that traced people for you. It took time, but they usually got there in the end, and they said that the majority of people weren't at all grateful for being found. It was this that stopped me from picking up the telephone now. I didn't want to walk into the room where Lynnet was and see her look cold and unfriendly. She was old enough to go off if she wanted, and though untrained at anything was quite clever enough and pretty enough to hold down a job. In the bright morning light I didn't think of her as a little lost kitten any more, but as someone who had always known very well how to get what she wanted. Joe could hurt her, because he had taught himself a devilish skill, but in the world outside the home Lynnet had been able to stand up for herself.

"Except where men are concerned," I suddenly found myself saying, as I drank my coffee. You know very well she's too innocent. Lynnet had not met many men; Joe had seen to that. But during my year at college and later Lynnet had fallen in love twice. From her letters, short and scrappy, I never knew what happened, but both love affairs had in the end made her unhappy. I suppose this was all right with Joe. A happily married sister wouldn't have suited him. I wondered even if he would have let her marry. I was willing to bet he would do his best to break it up.

I suppose it was something to do with a man that made her desperate, I said aloud, as I rinsed the coffee pot and put it away. Without warning, a rush of hot tears flooded into my eyes.

There was a part of my interview with Joe that I had suppressed even to myself. I had not left him after the revelation about his will. I had turned back, taken out my handkerchief and wiped his forehead where the beads of sweat glistened. He had let me do it, leaning back against his chair, staring up at me with eyes as big and beautiful as Lynnet's and a darker blue in the bargain.

"Can't we go back, Joe?" I asked. "Back to when we were friends and before you got so angry and I became clever and cold and hard."

"That's going back a long way. Too far for me. And you know why it happened."

I stared at him silently, wanting, somehow, to heal the wounds inside him. "I know it happened one summer. One day you turned on me and Lynnet as if we were your enemies."

"You became my enemies."

"It doesn't seem to me it was our fault," I said. "Anyway, not Lynnet's, perhaps more mine."

"I couldn't separate you and Lynnet," he said, turning away so that I saw only the profile with the lines from nose to mouth. "You were both young and female and beautiful. . . . I hated you. But I had my reasons."

"I suppose I knew," I said.

"Of course, Selina. Who could miss it? And so you ran

away. I don't blame you. It wasn't your fault, but it certainly wasn't mine. And I was being punished. I was eighteen, Selina. It's hard to be a saint at eighteen. I wasn't built that way. It's not in the blood. Goodbye, Selina, and don't ever come back."

I did turn to go as he ordered, and then stood for a minute at the door wondering how to say goodbye.

"Take your handkerchief," he said in a level voice. "Here, catch." He was quiet now, leaning against a cushion as if he was tired, all the anger and bitter laughter of a few minutes ago drained away.

I caught the little crumpled ball and then dropped it.

"Butterfingers." He said the old nursery taunt almost kindly.

"I never could play ball." I bent to pick it up. "Sorry."

"One thing you'd better learn about yourself, Selina. Clever you may be, but cold and hard never."

For a moment we stared at each other and then I turned away through the door.

I hadn't let myself think of this scene, but it all came vividly to life again now. I put my head on my hands and wept for Joe as I had not done before.

The little cat stopped me by jumping on the table and playing with my hair. Like all cats, she was no sentimentalist.

"You can't stay here, cat, you know," I said. "This is a furnished flat and the lease says no animals."

I ought to have seen the writing on the wall then and recognized what might have been the first of Joe's spells working out. Instead, I dressed and went off to the British Museum where they had a manuscript for me to read. I was dealing with a thirteenth-century murder case. As a case it was straightforward without being boring. An apprentice workman in London's Cheapside had murdered his employer and his employer's wife because of the harshness and savagery with which they had treated him. I imagine there must have been dozens of such cases over the years. This one interested me because the employer was a wealthy silversmith and the account in the plea rolls gave many interesting details about his household and its way of life. I learned, for instance, that a thirteenth-century lady of breeding used a little strip of fine linen called a foot lappet to rest her feet on after she had bathed them each morning. If she was lucky she had rose petals in the water in which she washed her feet. It would be wrong to think of those ladies you see looking out at you from a Memlinck or a Van Eyck as unwashed. Hands and face and feet, at least, were carefully washed, and in addition they probably smelt of sandalwood or clove or some other peppery perfume specially imported for them on the spice route from India. Men grew rich on this trade. Usually I found this sort of detail absorbing, but my intellectual self wasn't on top that day and instead I wanted to go out in the sunshine, feeling the air on my cheeks, so I did go out, and it was raining in Russell Square.

I wasn't prepared to meet Ted Lestrange in the garden of the square. He was standing there staring morosely at a quarreling group of pigeons and looking pretty cross himself in his London clothes.

"Whatever are you doing here?"

He looked up and without any perceptible lightening of his expression said: "I came to see you."

"Oh, go on, you didn't know I'd be here in Russell Square. How could you?"

"I was waiting. I know you work in the British

Museum Library. I was going to be on the steps at one o'clock when you came out for lunch."

"And supposing I'd worked straight through the lunch hour. I often do."

"Then I was going to send in a porter. One of those men in the smart uniforms who stand in the main hall. I was going to ask him to find you and bring you out."

"And what were you going to do when I was out?"

"I was going to ask you to lunch. With me."

"Oh." I considered. "I'd like that. But why? Am I business or pleasure?"

"Pleasure, of course." His stern expression didn't alter much, but he knew what good manners demanded. "Some business, too."

"Why didn't you just write a letter then?"

"Because you don't answer letters." He suppressed his irritation.

"Oh, that's true." I had remembered that little pile of letters.

He gave me lunch in a small Greek restaurant where I ate moussaka and drank retsina. I like the strong, rough taste which is as if a little amber had become liquid and seeped into the wine. I was eating green figs when he exploded his bombshell.

He leaned forward across the table and said earnestly: "I want you to go back to the States. You could, couldn't you? Dorothy Wigmore says her cousin could fix it."

"I'm sure she could. But I don't need things fixed for me. Why should I go?"

"We'll talk about that later. You won't go?"

"No."

"Then sell me Catt's Tower."

I was startled into a quick reply. "You're the second person who's asked me to do that."

"Really? Who else?"

"I had a phone call from a Cardiff estate agent. Said they were acting for a buyer. I said no. I can't sell until Lynnet comes back."

"If you sell to anyone, it had better be me," he said decisively. "Unless you're thinking of getting married. Are you thinking of getting married?"

"No. Not me."

"Girls usually do. It's a solution." He didn't seem happy about the thought, though.

"I'm not getting married."

"I don't want you to go back to Catt's Tower," he said. "I don't think it's safe for you there."

I stared at him.

He went on: "Doesn't it seem strange to you? Lynnet gone. Joe dead."

"I don't suppose there's a curse on it," I said slowly. "What about Joe?"

"I saw Joe the night he died. He was laughing."

"I dare say." I too had heard Joe laugh.

"I don't think he expected to die," Ted said doggedly.

I looked down at the red-checked tablecloth and instead I was seeing Joe's face on that last night. "He knew all about dying," I said.

"You've silenced me there." Ted finished his wine. I collected my bag and gloves.

"If you really think someone harmed Joe, then you ought to tell the police." I couldn't bring myself to use words like murder or killed.

"You forget, I'm the High Sheriff. I have my own ways of making contact with the police."

The office of High Sheriff passed from landowner to landowner. At one time Ted would have been the principal administrative officer of the Crown within the County. In fact one of Ted's forebears had been High Sheriff in the days when the office really meant something and had done so well out of it that the King threatened to hang him high if he didn't disgorge some of his profits. But those days were over, and now it was more of an honor mixed with a social duty. But there could be no doubt that it gave Ted contacts.

He insisted on seeing me home and waited while I parked my car and unlocked my door. The little white cat was at the door to greet me.

"This yours?" asked Ted.

"For the moment," I said. "Until I find it another home."

"I suppose you know it's deaf? White cats are always deaf."

"I'll teach it to lip-read."

The kitten jumped up onto a table by the door and stared at him from this height. A little low rumble came from the back of its throat. A pile of letters slithered to the floor.

"You ought to read your mail," said Ted, picking them up. "You'll find one from me there."

After he had gone I took his advice and opened my letters. Bills and receipts for the most part were what greeted me. A letter from an old college friend who had married. An invitation to a party. Two letters from America. The letter from Ted, which was a few lines asking for a meeting in London.

Finally there was a long letter with a typewritten address which looked so dull I had left it until last. It was so anonymous-looking that it might have simply been a circular addressed To The Occupant but, in fact, it was to me personally—Miss Selina Brewse, 23 Abingdon Court, SW3.

I opened it and found it contained a stiffish sheet of paper folded over once. I read it for a moment without comprehending what I saw. When I did grasp what I'd read it was like being kicked.

I was reading my own marriage certificate.

Believe it or not, I was a married woman . . . If you trusted the written word. As an historian, I was trained to do this.

There before me was the marriage certificate of Selina Joan Brewse, spinster, aged twenty-four, the daughter of what looked like William Brewse and his wife Mary Brewse. The flowing, elegant copperplate hand was hard to decipher, in spite of its grace. The marriage was duly witnessed by two indecipherable signatures. However, handwriting was my business and I did not despair of being able to decipher them if I really tried. It might be advisable to try very hard, I thought.

Two other facts had to be noted about my marriage lines. In the first place, what I had before me was a photocopy and not the genuine article.

And second, when the photocopy was made, a piece of white paper had been placed on the original over the bridegroom's name, and obscured it.

I was not to read the name of the man I had married.

I picked up the document and studied it again fruitlessly. A photocopy is a photocopy and you can't get much more than what it offers at first glance, however hard you study it.

My first impulse was to reject it utterly. "No," I said, pushing it away from me. "No." I wanted to tear it up or burn it, but I did neither of these things. Instead with the trained historian's feeling for a document I got a clean envelope, put the photocopy inside it, sealed it, and then placed the envelope in a drawer of my desk, which I locked.

My head was aching very badly and my eyes were blurring. I took some aspirin. I needed advice and didn't know where to go for it. I had lawyers, of course, but all the partners were brisk young businessmen to whom I was just an account.

I felt like running after Ted Lestrange and calling: "You were right, after all. I *am* married."

Only one thing stopped me. I didn't know whose name was hidden beneath the covering piece of paper. Perhaps it was his.

I suppose this state of madness lasted about five minutes, although it felt much longer at the time. Then the balance righted itself and I reminded myself that there was more to a marriage than a piece of paper. The bride actually had to be present. If I had been present, then the whole episode, from the ceremony to the bridegroom, had been erased from my mind. Things like that *could* happen, but I wasn't prepared to accept that it had happened to me.

I went to the drawer, and got out the envelope to study its contents again. It was still there. I wouldn't have been surprised to find that it had mysteriously disappeared.

The wedding had taken place at the Parish Church of St. Kenelm and the date had been June the fifth of this year.

On June the fifth I had been staying with a friend in America, convalescent from my accident. I had a way of checking too. I went into my bedroom, unlocked my dressing-table drawer where I kept my small amount of jewelry, and got out my passport.

I had left Kennedy airport on the twenty-first day of July. Somewhere in my passport there should be a date stamped. I flipped through the passport and soon found the stamps marking my entry and exit. The entry was clear and easy to read, October of the year previous, but the exit stamp was blurred beyond reading.

"Damn."

Never mind, I had my memory. My memory *was* me. And my memory talked with a firm voice and said that I had entered the country *after* the date on that marriage certificate. It added, moreover, that its records, carefully arranged, carried no impression of a marriage.

I put the passport away. I put the marriage certificate back in the envelope. Perhaps I should have destroyed the thing, but I couldn't bring myself to do that.

I did not sleep peacefully that night, or the next. My work did not go too well, either. It was nothing important; just a sort of roughness of the mind against which the details of everyday life seemed to catch, and which translated itself in physical terms into a sensation of unease. The days seemed very long, and yet I couldn't remember what I did with them.

Toward midweek I had the first of my appointments with the specialist, an eminent neurologist whose speciality, I had been told, was states of prolonged unconsciousness. I supposed that was why I had been referred to this specialist by my American doctor, although, in fact, I hadn't been unconscious for very long. "See the neurologist in about six months," the man in Boston had said. "For a checkup."

I had left it rather longer than six months and would probably not have gone when I did, but for the fact that the appointment had been half booked for me from the Harvard hospital. I was expecting a man, but the specialist was a tall slender woman with beautiful auburn hair. She wore a wedding ring and there was a photograph of a boy and girl on her desk. She saw me look at this, but she said nothing.

She did all the things that doctors do when they are checking your physical state and did them all deftly and neatly, and with a completely detached look, humming a soft tune all the while.

When she had finished, she still had questions. "And how are the headaches?"

"They have been bad lately."

"Aspirin help?"

"Oh, yes." It did when I took it, which I hardly ever did. I hate drugs.

"No double vision?"

"Oh, no, nothing like that."

She looked at me thoughtfully. "And your memory, how is that behaving?"

"I don't always remember to open my letters," I said with a little laugh.

She didn't laugh with me. "Not overworking, are you?"

"I'm not working at all," I said. "I can't seem to push on with it."

"How do you feel in yourself?" she asked.

"Different," I said tersely. "As if I was another kind of

person. As if something had happened to me." It was the first time I had put this feeling into speech and it was a tremendous relief to me. "Something has changed."

She nodded, as if she understood. "You're very tense. I'm not quite happy about you. I wish you to go somewhere quiet and rest. Have you somewhere you could go?"

There was a pause. "There is somewhere," I admitted. "I should be on my own, though."

She smiled and nodded. "It might be what you need."

When I got home I had one thing I wanted to do before I took notice of my doctor's advice. I picked up the telephone and booked a call for Boston. There was a time lag of two hours, they said, as the lines were busy. But I got the call before I went to bed.

"Hello?" It was my friend Rose in Boston. She sounded a bit surprised to hear my voice. And now I was speaking I did not know how to phrase what I wanted. It was ridiculous. How could I say: Did I leave your house at the beginning of June when I was convalescing from an accident to fly home and get married, and did I happen to tell you about it? "How are you?"

"I'm fine."

"You don't sound fine. You sound sort of wobbly."

"I'm thinking."

"A transatlantic telephone call's an expensive time to do your thinking. Any news for me?"

"No. What do you mean?"

"Well, I thought maybe that was why you were calling. That you were getting married, maybe."

"I don't know why everyone wants to marry me off," I said irritably.

There was a silence. Then Rose said. "This conversation doesn't seem to be getting anywhere."

I pulled myself together and produced a few items of gossip and information, hardly enough, really, to justify my call, but enough to cover up my motive. Rose played back very nicely, whatever she may have been thinking. She always had charming manners.

"When I was staying with you in the summer, did I go away at all, do you remember?" I said at last, plunging in.

"Not while I was there," said Rose pleasantly. "We had a happy time together. As you know, I was away for the best part of a week and you were on your own."

She may have been wondering what it was all about, she probably was, but she didn't say. That's what I meant by good manners. Rose would never embarrass you.

"Oh, yes," I said. "So you were. You went to give a lecture in Philadelphia."

"You hadn't *forgotten?* How is that memory of yours?"

"It seems all right," I said slowly. "Except for here and there."

"Well, you take care. Are you staying in the city? I think you should get away. Get some sun and air."

"I'm going to."

So the next day, with the white cat to accompany me, I drove down to the tower at Nun's Castle.

The tower seemed by no means welcoming, but then it never did. I hadn't expected to come back here so soon and there were no plans made to receive me. I didn't want any, I just wanted to sink anonymously into the place and be forgotten. Nor had I left any forwarding address in London, so with any luck there shouldn't be any letters. But I didn't count on this. People have a way of finding you out. Witness the kind soul who had sent me the marriage certificate. My flesh still crawled when I thought of it.

I had a box of provisions in the back of the car and I took them through to the kitchen. The place was empty and tidy, but that was about all you could say for it. It wasn't and never could have been anyone's dream kitchen. Everything in it was about thirty years old and just as I remembered it. The only new object was a refrigerator. In the old days we had managed without. I was glad to see it today, though, as the weather was still hot, although we were moving into autumn.

I hadn't told anyone I was coming. I knew that the news would soon get round, but I thought I would be left alone for a few days. Even then, people would be shy of intruding, especially the country people. They were a funny lot around here, quick to gossip, keen to embroider a story, but never eager to push themselves into your life. Lady Dorothy would, of course, eventually arrive with a bang. And Ted Lestrange would be downright angry. But I need not see much of Ted if I didn't want to. He wouldn't come unless I invited him.

It was strange to walk into the house and smell the emptiness. The telephone was working; I tested it at once. I wasn't quite mad. You need a lifeline somewhere. I had expected to sense Joe's ghost, but to my surprise there was nothing at all. The house was quite empty. He had paid me the courtesy of moving out entirely. One or two of his possessions were still around, but they evoked no feeling, no feeling at all. They might have been the books, chess set and drawing board of a stranger. In any case, I had never seen any of Joe's pictures. He had taken up painting after I had left. Lynnet had left even less around and this did not surprise me. Lynnet and I had learned early to be like snails and carry our homes on our backs. In other words we left about no testimonies to our interests, hopes or fears because to do so made us vulnerable, and experience had taught us that in this house soft spots got a knife in them. But Lynnet no more than Joe could efface all physical signs of her existence, so there were a few things she had used. On the back of the bathroom door was a bathrobe that was surely hers. It had been newly laundered and was fresh, but only Lynnet would have chosen that bright tangerine color. In the kitchen I found an old purse with the initial "L" on it and a few coins and a lipstick. I went into the bedroom we had once shared and found she had even left a few clothes. In a closet across the way was a coat in that coral color she loved. I left them hanging where they were for the moment. If she did come back unexpectedly I didn't want her to find herself all packed up and put away. Joe's things, however, I did gather together and put in a box. Lynnet had taken over the whole floor of the tower, made up of a bedroom and bathroom and the big closet where I had found her coat. After a moment's thought I left her rooms unoccupied and moved myself into a room on the floor below.

 I made the bed up with fresh linen I had brought with me. It was pretty stuff, new and bright, printed with red carnations. Somehow I wanted to wake up with my own things around me. But I was feeling surprisingly cheerful and rested; the house wasn't having its usual effect on me by any means.

 Perhaps the one dark spot was that I had packed the

letter containing the marriage certificate. A really strong spirit would either have thrown it out or left it behind. I hadn't forgotten it, either. I was trying very hard to push it to the back of my mind, but it wouldn't stay there.

Anyway, the good thing was I no longer believed in it. I had been the victim of a sick, sophisticated joke. It was too soon to laugh, but I might manage it one day. Meanwhile, although I was going to take a rest, as ordered, I had brought a lot of work with me, all of a very peaceful, academic nature and I dragged a table into the window of the big sitting room and arranged my books on it. Through the window I could see down the sloping turf to the belt of trees that stood between me and the river. What I was looking at had once been the moat of the old castle, and where there was now grass had once been a cobbled courtyard. Of the old castle only Catt's Tower, a corner of an outbuilding and a stretch of broken wall remained aboveground, although underneath there were various chambers and tunnels. We always called them the dungeons, but of course they were nothing of the sort and were much more likely to be storage chambers. Even now, after centuries of neglect, they were relatively clean and dry, and you could tell that grain and provisions stored in them would have kept for a long time. Once there must have been a well in the courtyard, but all trace of it had now disappeared. I had always meant to have a look for its site. I thought that a certain clump of bushes in the grass and somewhat to the right of the tower looked promising. I might try digging there; a little archeology would be amusing.

I was sitting happily arranging books and papers, enjoying tranquillity such as is known only by the convinced addict of the written word, for whom even contact with a page is sufficient satisfaction, when I heard Ted Lestrange's voice from the door.

"I suppose I ought to have known that to tell you to stay away was the surest way of getting you down here."

"I'm not really as perverse as all that." I stood up and turned to face him. He stood in the doorway with the big front door wide open behind him. "And I'm perfectly all right."

"If you're wondering how I got in, I had a key. I always had a key when Joe was alive, in case . . . well, it just seemed wise. Here, catch." He tossed the old-fashioned key toward me. "But as it turned out, when he was ill it wasn't any use. He was dead when I got here."

"*You* found him then? I hadn't realized that."

"Yes, I found him." He had come into the room and was standing looking about him. Giving me a brief glance, he answered the question I did not like to ask. "He was on the floor by his chair. As if he'd tried to stand up and slid down. That was all. I picked him up and put him on the sofa and got the doctor. But he was already dead."

"I'm surprised Joe let you have a key. He was so secretive."

"He didn't have much choice. The doctor told him there had to be someone. He used to telephone me every morning. The morning he didn't telephone I came across but it was too late."

I looked down at the key in my hand. "Perhaps you should keep this?"

"No." His voice was flat. "My responsibilities are at an end." He said it so clearly, he might have shouted it aloud.

And then, I had another thought. He was behaving

very oddly. He was being interfering and proprietary, which was not a characteristic of Ted Lestrange. Far from it, he usually gave the impression he didn't much care when he would see you again. In a way I'd always found this galling. Now he was behaving as if he had a duty (I sheered off the word *right*) toward me. Perhaps he thought he had. I could hardly go up to him and stare into what were, at the moment, rather hostile blue eyes, and say: Am I married to you?

I knew what he meant. As I had disregarded his advice I was on my own from now on, and needn't look to him for help. I made a furious vow inside me that I never would.

"How did you know I was back?"

"My dear girl, you were away so long you forgot what life is like here. You hadn't been here more than an hour before I received the news of your car having come into the valley. Within the next half hour I heard you'd taken the road up here and not through the village."

"And then you came over yourself?"

"It was a mistake. Clearly. I see that now."

"Oh Ted," I sighed. It was no good fighting with Ted; he was my nearest neighbor.

"I wouldn't have come if I hadn't known you were on your own," he said stiffly.

"Now what do you mean by that?"

"Nothing. But if you'd, that is, you naturally might have . . ." He was floundering badly.

"You thought I might have come down with a man," I said in a level voice.

"It's always possible you might be married," he said stiffly.

"You've been hinting that all along," I cried in a real fury. "What gave you that idea?"

He fiddled around with his coat for a bit, then said: "Joe did. The last time I saw him."

"*Joe* said I was married? He was mad. How could he possibly know?" I remembered Joe laughing and wondered if all that was happening to me was an echo of that laughter. "Joe was wicked. He was cruel. What would he care if I was married? He didn't care two pins for me. I'm glad Lynnet ran away."

"He was in love with you, as a matter of fact. I'm surprised you never knew."

"Then he had a very funny way of showing it."

"Yes," he said, without any expression at all. "People have, sometimes."

"I wish I'd never come back and seen Joe," I said. "I only saw him that once, after years apart, and only for about ten minutes, and I feel as though I'll never be the same person again."

He gave me a strange look, which I did not fail to notice. I met his gaze, so that he was forced to speak. "I didn't know that you'd only seen Joe on that night he died."

"Yes, just then." I still held his gaze.

"You see, I knew you were down here earlier in the summer, and I supposed it was to see Joe."

"I wasn't here."

He looked at me doubtfully. "Oh?"

"Or perhaps I came to marry Joe," I said, remembering the marriage certificate. "It would explain a lot." And there was a lot it would not explain, as well, but no matter.

"It's not true," he said at once. "And don't joke about it."

I didn't say yes or no. I thought myself it wasn't true, but I was leaving the matter open and I'd never felt less like making a joke. "Tell me why you thought I was down here earlier in the summer."

"You mean you weren't here then?"

"I've already told you I wasn't." I was getting angry again.

"All right. So you didn't come back and you didn't see Joe. It's your business." Clearly he didn't believe me. I felt like hitting him. He was walking toward the door, prepared to depart in anger.

"Tell me who said I did?"

He stopped and looked back. He'd never heard about Lot's wife. "Joe's nurse told my housekeeper that Joe had been talking about you." He added thoughtfully, "Now that you mention it, I suppose that's not much evidence. But you certainly seemed on Joe's mind this summer."

"Joe!" I said. "What a lot goes back to Joe. He told you I was married. His nurse told you I was down here on a visit."

"Joe was very perceptive sometimes. He picked up things in the mind."

"And what does that mean?"

We were getting into that quarrel whether I wanted to or not. Anyway, I thought, I had got one thing clear in my mind: I would not have married Ted Lestrange whether in a state of amnesiac shock or not. I thought it was a fair bet he would not have married me either.

"I suppose I meant he was clever and sometimes saw things before the rest of us."

It was a good answer, because it left me with nothing to say. Presumably he felt the same, because he left soon after, banging the door smartly behind him so that the little white cat jumped.

"You aren't deaf then, little thing," I said, looking at her and stroking her head.

I was brushing my hair for bed, already in dressing-gown and slippers, when I heard the first clear note of music.

I stopped, frozen into immobility, my brush in my hand. A woman was singing in the room below. She must have been singing for some minutes before I took it in, because she was in the middle of a phrase. I knew the voice without a moment's doubt: it was Lynnet's. I went to the door and stood there listening. There could be no doubt. It was Lynnet's own voice; she was singing a gay little song, "Cherry Rype."

> Cherry Rype, Cherry Rype,
> Rype, I cry.
> Full and fair ones, come buy, come buy.

As she got to these words her voice went just slightly flat, as it always did.

I wanted to giggle and cry at the same time. What a way to come home, singing "Cherry Rype."

Picking up my long skirts I ran down the stairs, calling out:

"Welcome, Lynnet, oh, welcome back."

I was in the sitting room with hands outstretched before I stopped, the words of welcome dying away on my lips.

No one was there at all. No one. The room was empty.

Only the little white cat sat on the arm of Joe's chair and looked at me enigmatically.

Even the singing had stopped.

I put my hand to my throat where a pulse was beating hard. "I didn't imagine the singing," I said to the white cat. Her eyes narrowed and she looked thoughtful.

Then I became aware of a soft whirring noise going on in the room, and then Lynnet's voice started again with the same song, only this time she was humming and singing in snatches. I realized I was hearing a tape recording.

Lynnet's voice stopped and there was a click. The tape had finished. I asked myself how it had ever been switched on.

It could only have been Ted Lestrange, but my mind steadily refused to accept this as possible. It was so out of character to play such a trick.

Then the white cat yawned, stretched and moved away. Where she had been sitting on the arm of the chair rested a small square of plastic with three buttons on it. Joe had had a switch to control his tape recorder from his chair. I stared at it speculating that the other two buttons were for the record player and television so that he could sit in his chair and manipulate all three as he wished. Presumably the little cat had somehow pressed a button.

My nerves steadied with the thought and I stroked the cat's head. She purred very quietly, but gave no other sign of appreciating my attention.

She jumped lightly to the floor with a little soft cry. I bent down to pick her up. She let me lift her easily. In spite of her aloof ways she enjoyed being petted. Her face turned toward me confidently, but my eyes stayed fixed on the carpet.

I was staring at a large fragment of torn fingernail. A man's fingernail, I should judge, a thumbnail, and bloodstained.

I didn't pick it up, or touch it. I walked away feeling sick and left it there.

Later that night I crept down and quietly brushed it onto a piece of clean tissue paper, folded the paper over and put the package away in a drawer.

I lay for a long while without sleeping. I had made a sort of challenge to myself in coming back to Catt's Tower and it looked already as though I should need to be strong to meet it. I wasn't sure if I had the sort of strength that was needed. Lynnet had not had it and she was gone. Joe had had it, but he was dead, and as a child the Tower had seemed to me to be full of selfishness and old treachery. I hadn't been wrong. I was sure of it now.

I was almost asleep when a strange quiet thought put itself into words in my mind.

In his last minutes of life, it seemed as though Joe had sat there listening to the sound of Lynnet singing.

Chapter Three

I slept badly, and the next morning I was sick. It wasn't at all what I had planned. I took my temperature but it was absolutely normal and I was obliged to come to the conclusion that the sickness was yet another result of my accident. There seemed no end to the surprises I had in store for myself. I dressed slowly and took my coffee to drink in an armchair by the big window which looked across the valley to the monastery ruins and beyond to Lady Dorothy's house. The sun was shining on the trees, now changing color in the autumn. I felt timeless. The landscape was empty and still. I felt as far away from the world as if I were on the moon.

I gave the house a perfunctory dusting (house-cleaning not being among my virtues) and decided to do some work to please myself. I would pace out the courtyard, try to find the site of the well, which must be there, and see if I could work out where the kitchens and pantries and butteries of the original castle could have been. There might be some clues left in the lie of the land and the disposition of the remaining stonework. The guardroom for the soldiers was surely Catt's Tower where we now lived. The living quarters of the Constable of the Tower and his family with their solar and retiring rooms had probably been placed opposite, with windows on each wall facing east and west, to get both morning and evening light. At the time when the castle was built the natural light of the sun was the privilege of the rich. The poor and servile lived in darkness, except when out-of-doors.

I put on a coat and walked out into the courtyard. I now felt splendidly energetic and cheerful; there was no accounting for my moods. Perhaps it was the idea of working. There was a brisk wind to pull at my hair as I stood on the grass. On my right hand was a low broken wall, then another at right angles to it. I fancied I could see under the rough turf the outlines of the two other walls which would have enclosed a small room. Here must have been the door. I walked through, and in imagination stood there, looking about. A few more fragments of walls suggested another room, and a still smaller one had led off it. There was a long flat stone showing through the turf in this inner room and I guessed it was a hearthstone and that I was standing in the kitchen—or one of the kitchens; the Castle probably had several, as it also had its own bread bakery and its own brewery. Plain food, no doubt, but good. It would need to be. Upon the quality of the victuals depended the spirit of the garrison.

Beneath the kitchens the cellars, one for wine and the other for ale. They were still in good order. Beyond them was the entrance to the so-called dungeon, and I thought I'd take a look at it.

There was a narrow stone passage and then two steps and you were at the edge of the pit. Joe had had electric light put in and the passage whitewashed, but the pit, or bottle dungeon, yawned below in blackness. It was dry enough, though, no smell of damp, which confirmed my idea that it was meant to store grain.

I looked down into the darkness. I suppose you could pop the odd prisoner down it too, if you wanted. I had a strange impulse at that moment, and acting on it, I went back into the house and got a flashlight from the kitchen and tied it to a length of rope. Then I came back and switched on the flash and lowered it slowly into the pit. It cast a small pale light, hardly strong enough to see much. But I could see that the dungeon was empty, which, strangely enough, comforted me a bit. (So I must have been expecting to find something there, just a rat, I told myself, and to find no rat was a relief.) Nor was there about the great hole the smell of humanity; it was wholly impersonal. Neither the stench of the living nor the breath of decay greeted me. But I could not see quite to the bottom, so that much of the question still remained to me.

"Lynnet," I called, suddenly and idly. "Lynnet, Lynnet." But there was only silence for answer. Of course, I thought, drawing away, why should Lynnet be at the bottom of a hole?

I walked away from the storage pit, to continue my search for the well which the castle must certainly have contained. I circled the courtyard studying the ground beneath my feet. Then I thought I saw what I was looking for. A circular irregularity in the turf as if something round had been covered up. It was a dark, rich green of weeds and grass. I pushed at it with my toe and underneath was a hardness like stone. I guessed this was the old well head, or what remained of it. Probably the well itself was long since filled in with earth and masonry.

It was while I was standing there that a sudden weakness and sickness swept over me. The sky faded, the color went from everything and grayness took its place. There was no keeping on my feet. I sat down on the turf and put my head on my knees.

So this is it, I thought, this is what my illness means, moments when the world retreats, when I am wrenched away from it by the loss of power in my own body. I felt as if I were bleeding somewhere.

I took one or two deep breaths and after a while I realized that the air smelled good and that the bad moment had passed. I was better.

Slowly I walked back into the house. I wondered if this was what the doctor had seen before me and if this was what mortal illness was. I imagined something growing and shaping itself within my brain pan; it seemed to me my sickness must come from inside my skull. My accident, apparently so trivial, was having serious consequences. I knew I had puzzled the doctors. It was as if it had created a second me, a sick twin, who went around living a life on her own. Wasn't Doppelgänger the German word for it?

The wind, which had earlier seemed bracing and cheerful, now seemed cold. I went back into the kitchen and prepared to drink the coffee I had neglected at breakfast. Perhaps it would taste better now. It hadn't tasted very good then.

I stood by the pot, waiting for it to reheat, always a

tedious process on this ancient stove. If I was going to be here much I would have to consider replacing it with something newer.

I was standing there waiting when I heard the sound of wheels on the gravel outside and a dog barking. Quick determined footsteps followed.

"Hello, Elizabeth," I said, without turning round.

"Heard you were back." A pleasant country voice, giving nothing away. But *I* knew the power was held in reserve.

"Everyone knows." I was calm. "I don't suppose I'd been back ten minutes before someone telephoned someone else. And once the operators know, everyone knows."

"You might have told *me*." There was no reproach in the voice. Elizabeth Meredith was too wise, too worldly and too old for that. I was looking at her now and seeing her, apparently unchanged; wrinkled, suntanned skin, white hair pulled back in a thin bun, eyes sparkling and young. On an impulse I went over and kissed her cheek, which was soft and smelling of some good clean healthy soap.

"Well, welcome back." She was studying me. "You've come back with a pretty face, but you're as thin as a rabbit, girl." She was ready for a gossip. "See many changes here?"

I shook my head. "Not so many as I expected." In some ways the countryside seemed changeless. "Except Lady Dorothy's hair: that's gone more golden."

Lizzie gave a snort. "It's a wig. They say she's got six, and they're all stuck on posts round her bedroom. And she's my age if she's a day. What would you say if I wore a wig?" She gave a happy hoot of laughter at the thought. "Still, you can do everything if you're rich."

"I suppose she is rich?" I said thoughtfully. Sometimes

wealth is crumbling quietly away behind a prosperous façade.

"Oh, rolling, dear. Six wigs, three cars, a secretary and a machine to copy her letters, now *that's* riches," said Lizzie confidently. "And likely to be richer too. We've had surveyors and men with instruments prowling round here. They've found something, depend on it. With her luck, diamonds."

The mongrel dog, her constant companion, was at her heels, eyeing me alertly. All Elizabeth's friends believed she only had to say the word and he would eat one up. He certainly had a splendid set of yellow teeth and liked one to see them, but to be fair to him, in all the years I had known him, and he was getting on now, I had never heard him say an unpleasant word. His breath smelt, though. I stepped back. "I've got a cat now," I said. "You'll keep the dog off him?"

"What, Sammy? He's as gentle as a lamb." She patted his sandy-colored rough head while he looked at me enigmatically. "I'm a lamb in wolf's clothing," he seemed to be saying. "It's how I operate; a good trade is done by all."

"And what have you come for, Lizzie? Apart from wanting to see me?"

"I've come to clean the house, of course." She was calmly putting on a starched white apron. "I've always cleaned the house except when Joe gave me notice in a mood of his, and even then I came in on the quiet and had a quick dust round. He never knew. Or rather, I'll say he knew and didn't choose to notice."

"It looks pretty clean to me," I said.

"You'd never notice. Head always in a book." She was selecting a duster from a cupboard. "Mind you, I shan't come regular."

"No," I nodded. Naturally Lizzie wouldn't come regularly: she kept you on your toes better if you never knew when she'd be looking in. I poured the coffee and drank it.

"Still drinking too much coffee, I see. That's what keeps you thin."

"I don't think so." I was no longer paying her proper attention, because the coffee, which had scorched my throat, was making me feel sick again. I stood there for a moment more, hanging on to my self-control, and then fled.

When I came back she was calmly mopping the floor and the white cat, who had emerged from some hiding place, was standing on the table glaring down at the dog, who was wagging his tail and still pretending to be a lamb while he showed his wolf's teeth. Puss very rightly paid more heed to the teeth, which looked sharp and shining, than to the wide false smile.

"Well, what happened to you?" said Lizzie.

"It was the coffee. Made me sick. My accident has made me funny like that."

"Well, it wasn't a motor-car accident that caused such sickness when I was young," said Lizzie. "But I suppose you know best."

It was the sort of remark Lizzie made all the time, she meant nothing by it, especially to me, whom she loved. It was the sort of joke thrown off easily by her generation of countrywomen. I rejected the thought at once, but it came back again and lodged itself in my mind. I remember going to the mirror in my bedroom and staring at my face and wondering. I seemed lost in a web, soft strands catching at me all the time so that I couldn't get out. But I stood there while I heard her words ringing through my mind.

What was the natural consequence of a marriage, I thought, but a pregnancy.

My body had been behaving badly lately. I had put this down, as, no doubt, had the doctors, to the shock of my accident. I think that there was some idea that the pituitary gland might have been affected. For the first few weeks of pregnancy there is little physiological change, the body holds itself aloof from the intruder, tolerating it, but no more. Then, suddenly, the cells multiply.

My mind rejected all these stories my imagination was putting forward as fantasy, but I knew I was stuck, that I couldn't get away from them and that I had to get hold of some hard facts.

Well, there was one way of doing it, you rang up a doctor, and you took a test and then you knew one way or another and God help you. Good news for some, bad for others, it depended on what your position was. I didn't know what it would be for me either way: a rather hilarious joke, only I wasn't laughing.

I could hear Lizzie banging around in the other room. I could ask her questions and get back sage, folk-lore answers, but I couldn't tell her in return what she would want to know. Where? When? And, of course, most of all, who?

What would she think of a girl who couldn't begin to think of a name? Lizzie wasn't a particularly puritanical character, no countrywoman is, but she would expect a name for the father of my child if I was going to have one. For that matter, so would I.

Then my nerves steadied and I began to giggle. It was a ridiculous position to be in, and I could see the funny side.

"What are you laughing at, then?" called Lizzie from the door.

"Myself."

"You don't laugh at yourself enough, my girl. You want to do it more often."

"You need a sense of security to laugh at yourself, Lizzie, and I haven't had too much of that."

"You have to pretend to find life funny," said Lizzie. "And after a while it comes natural. Remember that, my girl, when you start to feel sorry for yourself." And she returned to her work. No, there was no self-pity in Lizzie. "That's an improvement. Looked like a sick cat, you did, just now."

I didn't feel sick any more, I suddenly felt fine, and I could hear Lizzie banging around noisily in the room next door. It wasn't true either that she always cleaned here. She did it only when Lynnet let her, which wasn't all the time. Lynnet had thought it was time she admitted her age and rested. But Lizzie Meredith was not willing to admit to either her age or battle fatigue: because she was a warrior and her battles had been many and famous. She had gone into one hospital as a patient and had emerged having organized the nurses into a union and put them on strike. This was in the thirties, too, when nurses didn't have things like unions or strikes. They won then, and would have gone on winning if Lizzie had stayed in the hospital, but she left, and afterward they slipped back until another three decades dug them out again. Lizzie was in advance of her time. It wasn't that she cared anything for unions or had political ideals, she just liked to see everyone get their rights. I was one of her battles, an unfinished one, really, and I knew she hated to give me up.

"Heard from Lynnet?" she said suddenly, as she put her coat on to go. So that was why she had come. She too was worried about Lynnet.

"No."

"Silly girl, silly girl. Don't you be silly, Selina."

I shook my head. Silence on this was the best I could manage. I didn't think I was silly, but I might have been incredibly unwise.

"Because you've got your education that I helped you get." She paused for a moment and considered the notable battle in which she had organized my departure to school together with the money to pay for it. "And that ought to keep you out of trouble. And you've got a weapon."

I didn't say anything. She had her own myths and this was one of them, that education protected you, also gave you your license to kill. This, too, belonged to her generation. I knew better.

"But that silly girl, Lynnet," she grumbled. "Quarrelling with everybody and then going off like that."

"Did she quarrel?" I thought about it. "Who did she quarrel with?"

"Everybody," said Lizzie. "Joe, you, me."

"She didn't quarrel with me."

"You haven't heard from her, though. She had a silent quarrel. You know what she was like, she could withdraw right into her shell."

Lizzie was right. If Lynnet was hurt, she did sulk; it was only logical that feeling badly hurt, she should disappear. But the old childlike Lynnet had always come back, and returned charmingly eager to be friends again. I hoped the new Lynnet would.

"She must have had a big big quarrel," I said. "But why doesn't she come back now? It's lasted too long."

"I hope she's all right," said Lizzie in a quiet voice. She didn't look at me, as if she didn't want me to see the expression in her eyes. When she had a bad thought she hated to have you read it there. Lizzie always claimed she had second sight. I don't think she did have, but she was a good guesser.

I put my hand on her shoulder and pulled her gently round so that I could see into her face, then I looked into her eyes to see what was printed there.

Soon I looked away. I didn't care for what I had seen. In Lizzie's eyes was the message that she thought Lynnet to be dead.

"I always thought they'd go together," she said huskily. "Brother and sister. They were linked. Neither one could escape the other."

"Lynnet will probably outlive us both," I said. "She's a good strong healthy girl."

"Not inside she isn't. You are, she isn't."

"If she comes back I'm strong enough to save us both," I cried. I don't know what I meant by it, except that it was a gesture of defiance against fate, somehow. Lizzie seemed to think she had my fate and Lynnet's all bound up and waiting for us, and I thought I knew better. I might have a surprise or two for her. Fortunately she did not seem to notice what I said.

"She won't never come back," said Lizzie, and then she got on her bicycle and rode away, taking her dog with her. "Let me know if that sickness comes back. I'll fix some sorrel soup and say a prayer for you." She was gone, without having done much cleaning.

That was Lizzie Meredith all over. I did love her, but she was an old terror. She had appointed herself the witch of the valley, seer, herbalist and faith healer all in one, and she meant to carry on her duties.

I settled down with my books and tried to work. To my surprise I covered a lot of ground, and I knew why it was, too: I didn't want to think about the present.

But eventually, of course, I had to. There are some thoughts you can't push away. But this time round I was practical. I knew there were tests that could be done quite easily. I knew you could even do them at home for yourself, if you had the proper equipment. It would be easy enough to write a letter, have the materials sent (in a plain cover, as the advertisements so kindly suggested), and then get the answer positive or negative all on my own. I didn't see myself doing it, though, and believing in any discovery I made. I thought I'd rather go to a doctor and get it over quickly.

Not the local village doctor, though. He was a kind man, but an old one, and I would have to explain too much to him. With a stranger I needn't explain anything.

Whatever the upshot, however, I should feel a fool inside. I was considering this thought, and stroking the little cat, and wondering how to choose my doctor, all three actions being very easy to achieve at once, when the telephone rang.

An aloof voice said that Lady Dorothy would like to speak to me. I knew the significance of this voice. Whenever you were out of favor with her ladyship a certain formality crept in and Lady Dorothy removed herself one stage from you by putting her secretary in between. At more friendly times, the secretary, a quiet girl called Phoebe Miller, who also worked part time for several farmers around, including Ted Lestrange, was allowed to stay huddled over her typewriter. Indeed at such times the only thing she was allowed to do was type, Lady Dorothy preferring to run her life energetically for herself rather than pay to have it run for her. Phoebe herself never quarrelled with anyone but led a carefully neutral life divided among her various employers. Undoubtedly she knew most of the secrets of the valley. I always suspected her of having a quietly swinging time in the county town on her days off. She *must* have some private life somewhere. Dorothy said she was in love with Ted Lestrange.

"Hello, Phoebe," I said cheerfully. "Yes, I'll speak to her. I suppose I'm in disgrace?"

"She saw your car," said Phoebe noncommittally. "She saw you arrive. You passed her on the road. She waved but you didn't see her. It worried her."

"I suppose she's listening to every word you say?"

"Something like that," said Phoebe carefully. There was a pause and the noise of Dorothy pushing Phoebe aside and taking control herself.

"Hello, you naughty girl. Why haven't you been to see me?"

"I'll come now, Dorothy, if you'll have me," I said humbly. It was better to get it over. Anyway, I was hungry, and Dorothy had a splendid Spanish cook. I should return smelling strongly of garlic, but who was going to kiss me?

When I looked round her room as I entered I saw both Ted Lestrange and David Griffith. By the fireplace were a group of other men, most of whom I had known all my life. From the look of them they perhaps were the committee of the local Farmers Cooperative, of which I knew Lady Dorothy was chairman. No other women were present. Lady Dorothy preferred men.

It was funny standing there and wondering which, if any, was my husband.

Well, I could tick off one or two, I thought, as I

accepted a drink from Dorothy and stood there drinking it. Alan Barth was married and had twin sons. Derek Joyes was sixty and a widower and had never shown any more sign of being interested in me than I was in him. I think he had once kissed me under the mistletoe but that was about it. Edwin Middleton didn't like women and didn't pretend to: he was reputed to be in love with his horse.

Is it you? Is it you? Is it you?, I thought, flicking my eyes over the others. But, of course, it didn't have to be anyone in that room. It was as I was standing there, sipping my drink, and smiling sociably, that the thought that had been at the back of my mind all the time came and began to look important. Why hadn't I thought about it properly before?

If I did have a husband, then why wasn't he making himself known? What had happened to make him run into hiding?

He could be dead. He could be dead and buried.

"What's the matter with you?" said David Griffith, coming up. "You look pretty sick."

"A funny feeling," I said. "Take no notice."

I trusted him because he had no imagination and asked very few questions. "David, I want a doctor. Can you recommend one? I have to keep up some treatment I am having because of my accident." It was the first lie that came to my mind.

"There's old Williams in the village," he said, without much interest. "Do you all right, I should think."

"Yes. I know him, of course. I want someone younger."

"I don't know of anyone. You'll have to ask Dorothy."

"She's never ill," I pointed out. "And she hates ill health."

"She knows everyone, however."

Exactly, I thought to myself, and she loves to ask questions.

Another voice broke in. "You should try Timberlake in Peterschurch," said Ted Lestrange, who had heard more than I wished. "I've met him on the Managerial Committee of the County Hospital."

I lit a cigarette and considered. Dr. Timberlake sounded like the man I wanted.

"He's a very reserved, discreet man," said Ted, somewhat dryly. "I think you'll like him."

I flushed as I turned away from him. My old friend was too perceptive by far. Perhaps Dorothy was right and almost all my thoughts could be read in my face.

He hadn't finished with me. "You look a bit thin," he went on. "See this girl eats a good lunch, Dorothy." A glance at Dorothy's face convinced me that Ted had persuaded her to ask me over that morning. I almost walked out on the spot, but it was too late, the rest of the party were already going away and I was on my own with her.

Dorothy and I were served our lunch alone, although I thought David Griffith looked both hungry and wistful as he left.

"Cosier, just with us," she said, tucking her feet under the table and spooning up a rich fish stew. It was Friday. Lady Dorothy always ate fish on Friday, having first fasted and been to church. She kept to a set of religious observances which she claimed to be both pure and antique (her words) but which I suspect she had largely invented. I always thought myself that, if known about, they would have caused raised eyebrows in both the Vatican and Lambeth Palace. But Lady Dorothy's spiritual home was really Stonehenge although she didn't know it. She was a Druid priestess in disguise.

At all events her fish stew was lavishly flavored with saffron and garlic and was not austere in the least. On the contrary, after eating it, you felt replete and happy, which was, I suppose, a good thing in itself.

"And of course, you want to talk to me." I kept my face agreeable. "I suppose Ted Lestrange told you to?" Yes, it was written all over him. What did he say? Tell her to go away?

"I don't know what you've done to that man," she said. "I used to think of him as so calm. Now he seems to get upset as soon as he thinks of you."

"I hope not," I said soberly.

"He's ten years older than you, but I always used to hope that you and he might . . . But no, I suppose you wouldn't."

"I don't think so," I said.

"All the same, he's the only man in the valley who can hold a candle to you. Except Joe," she sighed. "Goodness, the quarrels you three used to have when you were children, you and Joe and Lynnet, just children's quarrels really, but you were so *deep* and serious. It was being on your own. From the age of about fourteen you hardly had an adult who could say you nay."

"I never felt orphaned."

"You were though, and it showed. Shows still, in you, Selina. You sometimes look as if you were all alone on a mountain peak."

"I do?"

"Yes. It can be frightening."

I smiled. "I've never frightened *you*, Dorothy."

"No." She smoothed her thick, still blonde hair. "I've worked hard to keep up with you, Selina. I think I can say that to you now." She poured some golden wine, sipped it, and considered me. "It's true Ted Lestrange wants you away from here. I don't know. Perhaps he's frightened of you."

"He wants me to sell him Catt's Tower and all the land."

"Mm," she nodded. "I know. I'd buy it myself if it were on the market." She looked at me questioningly and I shook my head.

"There's Lynnet," I said. "I can't sell without her permission. We own it jointly. That was a kindness Joe did to me."

"Don't be bitter."

"He knew I didn't want the place. That it would only complicate my life."

"What will you do with it then?"

"I'll give it all to Lynnet." I drank some wine, feeling mildly intoxicated. It wasn't a bad feeling, provided I didn't let it go too far.

"Do you think Lynnet will ever come back?"

"Why not?"

"I think she may have gone to join her father," said Dorothy quietly.

There was a minute filled with nothing but my breathing. Then I said: "I don't know what you mean?"

"Your father was killed just as you have always been told," said Dorothy deliberately. "But Lynnet's father was not."

I knew now that it was to hear this I had been brought to the house.

"As far as I know he isn't even dead. He was involved with a lot of extreme political activity. He put a bomb under a statue of Edward I in Cardiff. No one minded about that too much: it was a bad piece of sculpture. But then he planted a bomb in the old reservoir up in the hills because the water was drained toward the English Midlands. A policeman died there. This was years ago, remember, when bombs weren't so common. Anyway, he got out of the country and took refuge somewhere."

I was trying to take in what she told me.

"Where did he go?"

She shrugged. "I don't know which country took him in, but I suppose one did. He counted as a political refugee, no doubt." Then she added deliberately. "But I've always thought he kept in touch with Joe and Lynnet." She looked at me. "He's called Lynnet home."

"I can't believe it. Not of Lynnet. She was too straightforward. She had no secrets."

"Don't mistake simplicity for innocence. Plenty of people fell into that error with Lynnet."

"I think I have made that mistake about Lynnet," I said slowly. She had said something illuminating. Dorothy could be very wise sometimes. I saw now that Lynnet could not be as innocent as I had imagined; she must have had a secret because she had gone away. Even now she was living a secret life. The minutes were ticking away for her, she was growing away from us in her privacy, changing into someone we should not recognize. "You're right, Dorothy."

"You're such a *nice* girl, Selina." She patted my arm and gave me a warm smile. "So open, no secrets."

She was wrong there, I thought, it looked as though I did have a secret. It was so secret it was even a secret from me.

All the rest of the day I was quiet and worked. At night I cooked some food and ate it without much relish, but still, I ate it. I caught a glimpse of my face in a mirror and saw a face that was thinner than I remembered, with eyes big and shadowed. It was my face as I remembered it, and yet I looked different. I knew as I stared at myself that I hadn't lost in looks; that is, it suited me to be fined down like this. I remember turning away from the mirror, half-impressed, half-dismayed by my appearance. I did indeed look like a girl in a dream.

I gave myself a respite from my problems then and listened to music and read Jane Austen and then a gothic novel for fun until I fell asleep.

The next morning I looked up Dr. Timberlake in the telephone book and dialed his number. Autumn still hung over the valley and as I sat there at my desk, holding the telephone, I could see the richness and sweetness of the landscape spread out before me. The trees were turning color so that all the shades from gold to orange red were overlaid on the essential deep green of the background. In the distance, somewhere, a bonfire was burning and I could see its smoke drifting lazily upward. The sky was a clear bold blue of the color you see in Italian primitives but hardly ever in real life. It was the sort of day I love best, when just to be alive was happiness. Even now, puzzled and bewildered as I was, every sense was delighted in it and I felt my spirits rise.

The fall into what happened afterward was even more

sickening by comparison. I ought to have been prepared for shocks but I was temporarily off my guard.

I heard the telephone ringing in the doctor's office in Peterschurch. The telephone book had revealed that Dr. Timberlake's practice had several numbers so I guessed that it was a big affair, probably employing several junior doctors. Even the name of the house sounded grand: Tabard House. Wasn't a tabard the short surcoat worn by a knight over armor and emblazoned with armorial bearings?

The telephone was answered by a woman. "Dr. Timberlake's surgery," she said clearly. She enunciated the words precisely, as if she had trained herself to speak this way. Underneath I could detect a soft gentle slurring that was perhaps more natural to her.

I introduced myself. "Miss Brewse, of Nun's Castle, speaking."

"Oh, yes." Straightaway her voice seemed to have altered, with the careful control dropping away and the natural undertones coming up stronger. "What is it, Miss Brewse?"

She had my name clear at once. People often don't; it's an unusual name.

"I'd like an appointment with Dr. Timberlake, please. As soon as possible."

"Dr. Timberlake is very busy." It was possible I was imagining the slight coldness in her voice. I could hear faint movements. "I am looking at his diary. He could see you next week on Monday at ten in the morning."

"Oh, but this is urgent."

"If you could outline your symptoms, Miss Brewse, I could pass them on to doctor and he could judge if an early call is necessary."

Good job I'm not dying, I thought, my natural impatience rising easily to the surface of my temper. I controlled it. "I'd rather speak to the doctor himself," I said, coldly, in my turn.

"I'm a trained nurse, Miss Brewse," said the other woman patiently. I felt that the patience was assumed and that somewhere not very far away was irritation. "Won't you let me help you?"

"All right," I heard myself saying, the words suddenly coming pouring out. "You can help me. I want a pregnancy test. I want to know if I'm pregnant."

There was a silence which seemed to stretch on and on. You'd think a nurse heard that sort of thing often enough, but she didn't seem to have done.

"Oh, Miss Brewse! It is still Miss Brewse?" she said, and now her voice seemed sad. "Why not leave it for a while and see if the natural course of events won't answer you. Give yourself a chance."

"I want to know *now*," I said, my voice unnaturally strident.

"Now please, my dear, take my advice, try to take things calmly, give yourself a chance. I know how you feel . . ."

"No, you can't," I interrupted.

"But you don't want to turn into one of these poor neurotic women always imagining phantom pregnancies. You must control yourself. It really is up to you . . ."

"Let me speak to the doctor . . ." My hand on the telephone was shaking.

There was a pause of some duration this time.

I thought for a moment that no one was going to come and they were going to leave me there forever hanging on to a silent line. Then there was a click, and another voice spoke, a man's this time, Dr. Timberlake's, I supposed. He had a nice voice, gentle and rich and very soothing. But I didn't want to be soothed. "Miss Brewse? . . . It *is* Miss Brewse?"

I was silent.

"This is a completely private line, my dear. You need not be afraid to speak out," he prompted.

My voice was unsteady, but I managed to control it and speak. "I'd rather see you."

"I'm only trying to spare you unnecessary hopes. Or fears," he added softly.

"I don't know what you mean."

"But Miss Brewse, I examined you before your wedding and told you then that you have very little chance of conceiving."

I hung on to the telephone so hard that I could see the white bones of my knuckles showing through my suntanned hand. "When was that?" I faltered. No matter if he thought me a fool.

He stayed gentle, as if he was used to coping with hysterical women. "In the summer . . . I don't have the exact date in mind. You may remember at your urgent request I made it completely unofficial and kept no notes." He did allow a very slight note of dryness to creep into his voice at this point. I could hardly blame him. "But I did make clear that you would probably never have a child."

"But not impossible?"

"Nothing is impossible," he said shortly.

"Then I *must* see you."

I suppose the urgency in my voice got through to him, because he ceased then to be soothing, and said crisply. "I'll book an appointment for you at nine A.M. on Thursday morning."

"Thank you." I put the receiver down and stood there, shaking. The full significance of what both nurse and doctor had had to say was still sinking in. Both, in their different ways, had offered me shattering information. First, the nurse with her chilling advice not to turn into a "neurotic woman imagining phantom pregnancies," with the implication that she had already warned me against this obsession. And then, to make things worse, the doctor's clear statement that he had already examined me and found me almost certainly sterile.

How many times had either of them seen me?

I sat down on the sofa in the big window and lit a cigarette. Gradually the tumult inside my mind began to calm down. I relaxed, leaning back against the big soft cushions. I was shockingly tired. I put out the cigarette and closed my eyes; incredibly, for a moment or two I must have slept. And while I slept thoughts drifted and shaped themselves in my mind in the strange way they have. I could hear Dorothy's voice and she was speaking in that slightly shocked, slightly respectful way she had when some aspect of contemporary society made her realize she lived in the last half of the twentieth century and not the nineteenth, or earlier, which was her natural home. And yet no one knew better than Lady Dorothy how to fit herself out with the comforts of her own age. "Oh, the Peterschurch clinic," she was saying. "It's the abortion center for three counties."

"What am I doing going there?" I thought, and then, as a rider to the thought. "Did Ted Lestrange remember this fact when he recommended the place?"

Nevertheless, I worked for the rest of the day, hard and even with pleasure. The human mind does not care to dwell on reality for too long, and I suppose it was a sort of refuge to me to bury my head in my books. Perhaps I had been doing it all my life.

I was alone all day, but perfectly at peace. A sunny day was succeeded by a lovely night. I stood in the window of the tower and looked at the stars in the remote sky. I stayed long enough to be able to see a little of the gentle progress of the moon across the sky. I was smiling, I think, as I stood there, caught by the tranquillity and harmony of it all.

I wondered where Lynnet was, and if she were looking at the sky as I was. She hadn't been much of a stargazer in the past, and people don't change. Lynnet had always looked down at the flowers at her feet and not at the stars in the sky. Dear Lynnet, I thought, I don't think I ever quite appreciated your joyous common sense when we were together. I believe I took too much for granted.

I moved round my bedroom, rearranging my possessions. I had one or two very pretty dresses which were still gathering creases in my suitcase. They needed to be unpacked and hung up. I took out the first dress, the one I liked best. It was a soft clover pink and I had spent more on it than I could really afford. I shook out the skirt, it was a new enough dress to *have* a skirt after the era of the minis, and found a padded hanger. The hanger was an old one of which both Lynnet and I had been given identical sets for one teen-age Christmas. This one was covered with pale-pink padded velvet which matched my dress and was, I suppose, why my hand had reached out for it.

But I saw now that hanging from it, suspended by a thread of silk, was a golden circle. A wedding ring.

Without conscious thought I slipped it over my third finger on my left hand. It fitted perfectly.

I took the ring off and looked inside, there was no inscription, no date inside, but I wasn't the sort of person who wore rings with inscriptions was I? So presumably the man I had married wouldn't be that sort of person either.

I left the ring where it was, which you may think strange of me. But I was in no mood to feel possessive about wedding rings which might or might not be mine. I was a little mad just then, wild with all my expressible fears and hopes which merged one into the other so that it was hard to know where I stood with them.

That night, late, when the valley was quiet and the lights dim, Lynnet phoned for the first time. I heard her voice sighing softly across the wires. I was sitting by the telephone when it rang and so I picked it up straight away. There was a silence and I could hear breathing and I knew it was Lynnet at once before she even spoke, and I said so.

"Lynnet, Lynnet, is that you?"

"Yes, yes, it's me, Lynnet." I could hear her voice, soft and girlish. I'd forgotten or perhaps never noticed through sheer familiarity, what a musical local accent lay in the background of her voice. Telephones always accentuate that sort of thing. Probably it was there in my voice too, before I went away and became a stranger.

"Where are you?" I demanded. "This is Selina."

"I know," she said huskily. "I guessed. You've come home."

"But Lynnet, why did you run away? And *where* are you?"

"Oh, I didn't run," she said, "not really . . . I . . . I was persuaded to."

I could guess what that must mean; she sounded a bit self-conscious and silly. A man had persuaded her to go and perhaps she was now regretting it.

"Well, come home now, Lynnet," I said reasonably. "I want you. You know about Joe? I suppose that's why you are ringing?"

I heard her soft sighing "yes" down the line. I wanted to think she mourned Joe a bit. I myself was beginning to regret him more and more with every day that passed.

"So come home soon, Lynnet."

"No, I can't come home." She sounded very far away.

"Speak up Lynnet, this is a very bad line. Why can't you come home?" I asked sharply.

But there was no answer. Just a distant humming on the lines and then not even that: the line was dead. We had been cut off. I buzzed the operator and got only the reply that if I put the receiver down my caller would probably ring me again.

She did not. There was no further call from Lynnet that night.

Chapter Four

The white cat and I breakfasted together, sitting in a patch of sunlight in the kitchen. If I stayed here I should have to do something about the garden, I thought. But I didn't want to stay. Nor would I. Lynnet would ring again; she would come home (she'd *better,* I thought crossly), and we would sell the house. I didn't know what would happen to Nun's Castle, but it would no longer be mine. This was how I wanted it. I wanted to be outside.

Meanwhile, I was inside and Nun's Castle was my responsibility. I tidied the kitchen, and even polished the old-fashioned red-tiled floor. The cat watched me patiently, paws delicately together, tail curled.

I made her comfortable in her basket before I left her. All the time I was listening for the telephone to ring.

When it did I was surprised to hear Ted's voice. He

punctured my precarious calm. It's always what you're not expecting that gets through to you.

"Any news?" he said. It was his way of beginning a conversation on the telephone. It meant: tell me what's important quickly and let me go away again.

"No," I said cautiously.

"I'd like to see you."

"Later today," I said, even more cautiously. "I've got some work to do." And then, because, after all, he had rung me up and Ted Lestrange always had a good reason for what he did, "Have *you* got any news?"

"I think I might have. That's why I'd like to see you."

"Lynnet," I said. "You've seen Lynnet."

"No, no, I haven't done that. Don't jump to conclusions. I've found out something, that's all."

"She telephoned here last night."

"She did?" He sounded surprised, more, he sounded incredulous. I didn't like that note.

"Yes, she did. We spoke for a few minutes."

"Then you know more than I do," he said; he sounded grave. "Where is she?"

"I don't know," I had to confess. "We got cut off before she could tell."

"And she didn't ring again?"

"No."

"Did you tell her to come home?"

"Yes."

"Well, what you are saying makes my news small stuff. But I'd still like you to know." He sounded worried, more worried than before I had spoken. "Will you come to me this evening? Could you come about six?"

We left it at that. I was puzzled by the undertones in

his voice. They spoke of more than ordinary suppressions and editing of what he could have said to me. This might have been for my benefit or for other ears. We both knew the operator listened on the line. It was one more worry to take with me to Peterschurch and Dr. Timberlake.

I remembered Peterschurch when I arrived there. It was a pleasant small town, still keeping its own character in spite of the fringe of new building estates. I noticed that all the new houses were unobtrusively expensive, just as the older eighteenth- and nineteenth-century houses in the town center were elegantly painted, with windowboxes still displaying autumn flowers. I remembered someone, probably Dorothy, telling me how much sought after was property in this whole area. I could see why.

I had to find Dr. Timberlake's Medical Center, of course, but even this proved unexpectedly easy. In the marketplace where I parked the car, there was a map of the town with places of interest clearly marked. All the doctors' houses, of which there were a good number, as you would expect in so prosperous a town, were marked. I had only to follow the directions and I could walk there.

You know how it is when you are facing an experience you would rather put off: your legs become leaden, there is a heavy feeling in the pit of the stomach, and the throat muscles tighten. I had all of these symptoms and a few others besides. I am a coward, and I know it, but my particular type of cowardice takes the form of wanting to get the thing over quickly. I don't want to put a terror behind me; I want to be there, facing it. So now I hurried.

I stood for a moment looking at the long low

white-painted house lying back on its own sleek lawns before I rang the bell. The nurse who admitted me was elderly, and I knew as soon as she spoke that she was not the woman who had admonished me not to be neurotic. This woman's voice was quite different and much more friendly. I felt a little of my tension relax.

I was asked to wait in a small room with chintz-covered chairs and matching curtains. Two small birds fluttered in a cage, colored fish swam lazily in a heated tank. A large and sweet-smelling bowl of roses stood on a well-polished table. The whole effect was of a living room in a pleasant country house. I sat down and started to breathe more freely. Somehow, I knew that whatever happened to me in this house, it would not be bad.

I sat for five minutes and then the nurse came back and smilingly, but silently, led me from the waiting room across the hall and ushered me into a large room full of sunlight.

I took a step into the room toward a man who rose from a desk. He was slender and dark-haired. His kind brown eyes met mine and he smiled. I knew in that moment that not only had I never met him before but that he had never met me. You can't disguise or mask the look by which stranger greets stranger.

In all the circumstances, it was a moment of considerable relief. I didn't say anything, but I felt myself relax.

I waited for him to say something.

He frowned slightly and looked at a page of notes he had on the table, and then pushed them away from him, but he said nothing, just motioned me to sit down, and then waited for me to speak.

After a pause, I started to speak, and then he held up a hand and said gently that he must get my name and certain particulars on paper. He was being very clever and giving nothing away. I suppose doctors learn to do just that.

I, for my part, although anxious to be explicit about my physical state, was not prepared to go into my nightmare of a forgotten marriage. I didn't think he'd ask me *how* I came to think I might be pregnant and he didn't.

Once he started to talk, however, his questions were pertinent and searching. At the end of having listened to my account of my symptoms and heard my self-diagnosis and noted the answers to his questions, he leaned back, his calm unbroken and said, "You were right to come and see me."

I waited. I knew how to hold my tongue.

"I won't give you a physical examination. It might not reveal anything."

Except if I'm a virgin or not, I thought rather bleakly, but I naturally did not say so. It's the sort of thing one is supposed to know about oneself.

"But as you will know there is a very simple test we can make." He smiled at me in a detached, professional kind of way.

I nodded.

"Well, we'll do that. You will see the nurse on the way out and she will make all the arrangements, and in a very short time you will have positive or a negative answer."

He sat behind his desk, perfectly composed, and in charge of the conversation, but waiting, I suppose, for me to get up and say thank you and go. However, I had something else to say. I allowed myself time to think. I wanted to get the words right.

"When I telephoned to make my appointment," I said, taking the words slowly so he could get their full weight, "I got the impression you thought I had visited you before."

He was silent, but he looked thoughtful.

"In fact, I more than got the impression," I went on. "I think you actually stated it."

"A mistake, for which I apologize." He smiled briefly.

"I can't help wondering why you made that mistake," I said. I could see he didn't want to answer. He looked troubled, but he kept his mouth tight shut. "I feel in a way I've got a right to know."

"I don't think I can help you," he said, and he reached out his hand for a bell that was on his desk. I put my hand out and gently covered it.

"You did think you had seen me before, didn't you?" I went on remorselessly. "Until the minute you actually looked at me and then you knew you hadn't. Why was that? What is there about me?"

There was a very long pause, while he sat looking at his hands. He wanted the whole conversation closed, he wanted me out of the room, but he couldn't quite do it. There was some reason that stopped him. I thought if I waited silently, patiently, reason might win.

Finally he raised his head. "I will talk to you. Yes, we will talk. I will look at my diary and suggest a time. I have your telephone number?"

"Yes," I nodded.

"Six thirty, the day after tomorrow. You will be my last appointment."

I saw the nurse outside about my own matter and made my appointment for the next day.

Lunch with me and the cat was quite a gay meal. I was beginning to feel more myself. All right, so I'd been a little mad, but I was getting on my feet again. We shared a mushroom omelet. I got most of the mushrooms and the cat got most of the egg. She left me all the salad. Her sex, previously in doubt, had suddenly declared itself with the appearance of a rangy old tom from the farm down the valley. He, at any rate, had no illusions about her sex and so I decided to call her Mary. Mary is a good name for a pale little cat with yellow eyes.

Together we went out and continued the archeological study I had made earlier. I thought that with some more work I could map out the whole of the ground plan of the castle. There must have been *two* solars or upper living rooms, I decided, one facing south and the other west. The remains of the west-facing room were still extant. I could see the bricks of the fireplace and the beginning of an angled chimney rising above it.

All in all, I had a peaceful, tranquil day, better than I'd expected. Lynnet didn't ring. Every minute I thought she would and I rehearsed what I would say to her, but she never did.

At the back of my mind always I had the knowledge that I was going to see Ted Lestrange that night and hear something about Lynnet. I forced myself to be patient and wait, although my real impulse, as with the doctor, was to say: Tell me now, this instant. Patience has never been my strongest characteristic, whereas Ted Lestrange could, I knew, bide his time. He baffled me in some ways. He was older than I was, and had always been a commanding figure in my life. I suppose those few years were enough to give him a sort of authority. In any event I recognized his power while sometimes making vigorous attempts to assert myself against it.

I had given up archeology and was sunning myself and smoking a cigarette when I heard a voice behind me.

"Selina?"

I turned quickly: it was David Griffith.

"Griff," I said, reverting to the name of childhood. Sometimes we'd called him Griff, sometimes Prince David, the latter derived from a game we played as children in the ruins of the castle. We used to plunge up and down the piles of masonry, pretending to be royal armies. I never got a leading role; David Griffith and Lynnet grabbed them. But I think my interest in historical matters started then, because I began to try to work out the pattern of real battles, borrowing books from the County Library and studying the contours of the map. The place we lived in fed my imagination. The castle had known many skirmishes, some bloody.

"Selina, let me help you. There is something wrong, isn't there?"

I hesitated. I was tempted to tell David everything (a temptation I never had with Ted Lestrange) and throw all on his broad shoulders.

"Come on—I have a right to know."

It's come at last, I thought, he's going to claim me, he's going to say, 'But Selina, I am your husband.'

"You've always been someone special to me, Selina," he went on. "You and Lynnet. Like princesses. I was just the boy from the farm over the hill and you lived in the castle."

"Some castle," I said, divided between laughter and tears.

"It has its place in history. You, of all people, ought to know that."

"Don't idealize me," I said.

"No, I don't do that." He gave me a grave look. "I value you for what you really are."

"Oh, David." I was touched and yet dismayed by this innocence. Can one human being know what another really is? How could he know when I hardly knew myself. "I'm not sure if I'm so nice."

"Nice?" His face broke up into a smile. "What has that got to do with it? What you have is more valuable than niceness."

"Is it? I wish I could believe it."

"Oh, yes, it's your heritage, you see; nothing can rob you of it. You are you." He made it sound important.

He put his arm round me. It felt warm and comforting. I remembered how kind he had always been to injured or frightened animals on the farm. Once I had seen him hold a thrush with a broken wing tenderly in his hands and stroke its head with soft fingers. His hands had not changed. They were still gentle.

"I *am* worried over several things," I admitted. "One of them is Lynnet. The other is Nun's Castle. It's a responsibility, David."

"You're on your own and you're frightened, aren't you?" he said.

"Yes, I am and I don't know why." The acuteness of his perception surprised me.

"I could buy you a dog," he said, looking at me with sympathy and amusement.

"I have a cat." I drew away and straightened my hair. I felt better. He *had* comforted me.

He came and sat down beside me in the sun. "How are you?"

"I'm fine." I was suddenly aware that I felt marvelously

full of pride and a quick temper. But how much, looking back, had come from my own observation and how much from Lynnet? She had talked to me about him. I remembered this now, although I hadn't thought about it for years.

He saw the doubts gathering in my eyes, and started to put out an apologetic and friendly hand. I met it halfway.

"Welcome back, Selina," he said, holding my hand tight. "Stay with us this time, will you?"

He had a good way of holding hands, so that my own felt warm and secure inside his. I remembered he'd always had the gift of command and perhaps this was why we had always given him the part of Prince or Leader in our games. I let myself relax and enjoy the moment. I like to think I can stand on my own feet, and so I can too, but for a little while it was nice to pretend I was a different sort of person. Lately I had begun to think I might *be* a different sort of person. There seemed powerful emotions hidden beneath my tight, well-controlled skin that I hadn't suspected. Only in Nun's Castle could all this part of me spring to life, like one of those paper Chinese flowers that you put in a glass of water and watch open out. It could be why I had run away in the first place.

He let go of my hand and said, "I don't believe in love at first sight, do you? I think it grows slowly and quietly inside you; if it seems sudden, it's only because there has to be a moment when you first notice it."

I turned my head aside because I didn't want him to see the sudden springing of tears in my eyes. "It's different for everyone, Griff," I said.

A bell began to chime; I could hear the notes floating delicately across the valley.

"What's that?"

"It's from the chapel." He pointed to the chapel across the valley. "Lady Dorothy had a bell put in. It's old Harry ringing it, I expect. He rings it occasionally because he enjoys the sound."

"Old Harry?" I frowned.

"Yes, you remember him. He used to be Lady Dorothy's gardener. He kept an eye on this garden here too." He looked around where we sat. "Doesn't seem as though anyone does much here now."

"But why does he ring the bell?"

"He's a bit dotty now, poor old boy, and it gives him pleasure. He likes the noise. No one minds." He turned to me. "You don't mind, do you, Selina?"

"No." In fact I was glad of the bell then; it had broken up a moment I wanted ended. "No, if that's what he wants from life, who am I to interfere?" I ended.

"And what do *you* want from life, Selina?"

"Well, I don't know. It wouldn't be easy to say just like that."

He smiled and shook his head at me. "Back here at Nun's Castle we always say you know exactly what you want, Selina."

"I thought I wanted freedom," I said.

"That's just what you can't have because of what you are."

I was puzzled. "And what's that?"

"If you don't know about yourself, Selina, I can't tell you."

I was still considering this statement when he left. I suppose he meant that a woman of my character and ambition could never be free from the pressures her own aims put upon her.

I looked at my face in the mirror above the dressing table and wondered if it was so. I put my lipstick on and then took it off. What did it matter how I looked for Ted Lestrange?

Ted was not alone when I walked into his living room. The big front door stood wide open and I had let myself in. He was standing there talking to a tall, thick-set man who was a stranger to me. I thought he had an antiseptic professional manner.

Ted gave me a drink, barely pausing to ask me if I wanted one and certainly not pausing for an answer. Then in a preoccupied way he introduced the man as John Mallard. "Mr. Mallard works for an organization which specializes in finding missing people."

"Oh." I sipped my drink, which was a fine sherry, as you would expect with Ted Lestrange. He never had much money to waste, but he never bought the second-rate either. He had the best or went without. I didn't ask who Mallard was trying to trace. Lynnet, of course. I did ask myself *why* and what business it was of Ted Lestrange's. I dare say my eyebrows rose slightly.

"I'm executor under Joe's will," Ted reminded me smoothly. "I have an interest in finding your cousin."

"If you leave her alone she'll come back herself."

"Perhaps. But we don't want to wait too long. The estate's got to be settled. Especially if you decide to sell."

There it was again: the talk of selling Nun's Castle. I hadn't wished to become the owner of an estate, albeit a rundown one, but I would not be nagged into selling it. I felt the muscles of my jaws tighten and knew my face had taken on an obstinate look. I saw it reflected in Ted Lestrange's face. He sighed.

"Have you found Lynnet then?" I drank my sherry, enjoying the flavor.

"No."

Something in his voice made me look up. "What is it then?"

"Mr. Mallard has found a suitcase belonging to Lynnet in a railway luggage checkroom."

"Where?"

"Hereford."

"I didn't think you could leave a case for as many months as she's been away," I said. "Not without someone making a fuss."

"You can't. She made a special arrangement. Tipped the man in charge. Said she'd be back in a month."

"She's been gone longer than that," I said, fingering my glass.

"He kept quiet for a long time. Then he began to get worried. He told me when I came asking." This was Mallard speaking for the first time. He had a pleasantly neutral voice. All the same, I didn't take to him much. He looked as though he could be tough when necessary.

"So Lynnet left a suitcase, saying she'd be back, but so far she hasn't appeared?"

"That's the position."

"So either she's forgotten it, or she never really meant to come back or else she just hasn't been able to get back. Knowing Lynnet, I think I would say she means to return." Lynnet did not have many possessions and she had always shown a certain tenacity in clinging to them. "What's in the bag?"

He shrugged. "The case is locked."

"Oh, come on, you've opened it, surely you've looked."

But he wouldn't admit it. I stood up. "I want to see this case." From the look that passed between Ted Lestrange and Mallard I knew this was why I had been brought here. I was cross. I hate to be manipulated, especially by Ted.

"If anyone has a right to look, you have," he said gravely.

The drive to Hereford was quiet. I sat beside Ted as we drove through the curving lanes where autumn was beginning to touch the leaves. The sky was still a brilliant blue. It was puzzling about the case. I wondered what Lynnet was up to and why she was playing hide-and-seek. It wasn't behavior typical of the Lynnet I knew, except when she was frightened. Lynnet could be frightened quite easily, she was not a brave person. She was someone you wanted to look after and protect. Looking at Ted's bleak profile I supposed this was how he felt. I'd been away so long. Perhaps there *had* been something between the two of them.

"Is Lynnet running away from you?" I said suddenly.

He drove smoothly on. "I hope not." He didn't take his eyes from the road or relax the speed. But inside him something had winced. I knew it, and he knew that I had noticed it.

"She's running from someone or something," I said.

"Or running *to* someone," he said. "Have you considered that?"

"Lady Dorothy has." And I told him of Dorothy's theory that Lynnet had gone to join her father, had been summoned to join him, you might almost say.

"Nothing in that." Ted sounded surprised. "Brewse never took much interest in his children when he lived with them; he's not bothering now. He did have his own peculiar brand of politics, I admit that; he was a nationalist looking for a nation." He paused. "I can remember him talking, even now. He had a persuasive way with him, you had to stop and listen. Bright, pale eyes and an enormous head. A sort of bear of a man, and a beautiful voice. All his love went away from him, though, into causes and dreams."

"Lady Dorothy says he went behind the Iron Curtain."

"No one knows where he went. No place for someone like him in a communal State. If he *did* go to the East he's dead or put in prison."

"I wish I remembered him better. I just recall his voice."

"Yes, you wouldn't forget that voice easily. In a way the voice was the man. He hypnotized himself into thinking he was a sort of prophet." Ted swung the car neatly round a corner and we had arrived. We walked across the station courtyard to an office.

A sweet-faced old countryman, hardly plausible as a railway official, let us into a small room and showed us a small fiberglass suitcase, striped blue and white. It looked new and fresh and untraveled. It was also just a little bit more expensive than I would have expected Lynnet to be able to afford. As I looked at it, I felt as if it represented a small extravagance on Lynnet's part. It didn't look at all the sort of case she would leave behind and forget.

"How can you be sure it's Lynnet's case?" I asked. There was no label, not even an initial anywhere.

"I recognized the lady's face," said the railwayman, his voice soft and musical with rustic sounds. Shakespeare never came so far west, but so his contemporaries might have spoken. Perhaps Milton's Comus did speak so sweetly.

"Also, I did take a little money off her." He seemed sad and shamefaced that he had done this. "But I have been a little worrit that she never came back to claim the case."

Ted introduced me and explained I was the lady's cousin. I don't know how Mallard had overcome his initial scruples, which I am sure must have been many, and got permission to open the case the first time, but he made no fuss now when Mallard produced a small bunch of keys and selected one.

The case opened easily. At the last moment I felt a pang at disturbing Lynnet's property and cried, "Oh, no," but it was too late, the lid was up.

The case was full of neatly folded and packed clothes. I hadn't seen Lynnet for years. I didn't know what she had in her wardrobe, but from what I could see they looked the sort of thing she would choose. To one side was a square wooden box that I recognized at once: it was the box in which the tiny furniture for the doll's house was packed when not in use. I opened it. The lid fitted closely, just as it always had, and there was the usual struggle to pry it free.

"We always packed the furniture in here because it kept it safe," I said. Neither Ted nor Mallard answered. I could understand why.

Every tiny piece of furniture was broken, each chair, each table, each piece of fragile elegance deliberately broken in two.

We closed the case and left it there and went back to Nun's Castle. The drive was silent. Mallard was clearly not one for speaking freely unless he was being paid for it, and I had a lot to think about. Whichever way you looked at it the evidence presented by the case was disquieting.

"I wish we hadn't opened Lynnet's case. What we found was ugly."

"It's hard to know what to make of it," Ted went on. "After all, what is it, a box of broken doll's furniture? Perhaps she broke them herself."

"No," I said.

"Joe may have done it. He had the temper."

"Yes, it could have been Joe. It may have been the last straw. The reason she ran away." I could picture the scene: Lynnet in tears and Joe, his face stony, snapping the delicate objects in his fingers, one by one. "She would never have stopped him. Never have been able to, never, in a way, have wanted to."

"Are you telling me Lynnet was some sort of masochist?" said Ted dryly.

I said slowly, "I think she associated love and pain. We all did in Nun's Castle."

He drew his breath in sharply. "You hate it here, don't you?"

I nodded. "If I think about it. I haven't let myself think about it lately."

"Then sell it."

"You know I can't do that without Lynnet."

"There might be legal ways round that problem," he said cautiously. "I'm taking advice."

"But Lynnet herself will come back," I protested.

"Do you really think so?" He sounded grave. He moved his head round to get a look at Mallard, sitting taciturn and unmoving at the back.

"Why did you get me to come and look at the case?" The demand to know this had been rising uncontrollably within me all this time.

"In the first place, you are Lynnet's nearest living relative," he said patiently, "and you therefore had a right, perhaps a duty to go and look, and secondly, to prepare you for what might be to come."

I stared at him.

"Mallard's had a lot of experience with this sort of case."

"What sort of case? What are you trying to tell me?"

"Lynnet may have killed herself. She may have committed suicide."

I found I was too horrified to speak, the words went thick and then dried up in my mouth. Lizzie had hinted at this too. Perhaps the old countrywoman knew something I did not.

"It's part of the pattern," said Mallard. "A quarrel with her brother. I've seen it before. It does happen, miss."

"Not Lynnet. She has too much to live for." But even as I said it I wondered if it was true. In any case, it isn't what you've really got, but what you think you've got that counts, and who knew what Lynnet saw ahead for her? "In any case, I've spoken to her; she telephoned me. I told you."

Ted was silent. "Are you sure about that call?" he said, finally.

"Do you think I was imagining it?"

He sighed. "Not imagining, Selina, but you do want to hear from Lynnet, don't you? You may have jumped to the conclusion it was she on the phone, just because you wanted it to be."

I was angry with him, but he had planted a doubt in my mind.

"I think she said she was Lynnet." I was trying very hard to remember if my caller had said so. I had an uncomfortable feeling that it was I who had cried out, "Oh Lynnet, it's you?" "I'm sure it was Lynnet," I said.

"Are you?" He sounded unhappy. "I wish I were sure. If she calls again, call me at once, will you?"

Mallard cleared his throat hopefully. He was like a great big dog waiting for a bone. Then he asked for the bone.

"I could fit a bug on the telephone, just a recording device, Miss Brewse, and then we could play it back at leisure."

I turned my head to look at him. He seemed perfectly composed and harmless, though I knew he wasn't harmless at all, but immensely tough and professional. He had neat blunt features, but nature had turned him out bare of any expression whatever, except a sort of bland neutrality. "I suppose you were a policeman before you went into private work?"

"Yes, I was."

"That's all right, Selina," said Ted impatiently. "You can trust Mr. Mallard."

"Oh, I do," I said, thinking to myself that what I meant was that I trusted him to do his job coldly and well. I wondered if he had a wife, and what she thought of Mr. Mallard at home. I wondered if he had a child and played with the child. I was sure he did have a wife and she probably loved him very much. "But it is surely not necessary to go as far as that? Nor can I believe it will help bring Lynnet home." My voice was cold. I hated them both at that moment with a deep instinctive hatred which, looking back, seems totally explicable.

I saw a look pass between them. Mallard gave a slight smile.

I pondered. "I mean—it's not that sort of predicament—it's private, personal."

"We'll leave it then," said Mallard. He was perfectly polite, but something in the glance he gave Ted made me wonder which of them was really in charge. Ostensibly Ted had hired Mallard to do a job, but in that flash Mallard had given the impression he would not be easy to control.

"You will indeed," I said sharply.

"Of course." He got out of the car and held the car door for me to get out.

Ted got out too and walked with me to my door. It was propped open, as always with us at Nun's Castle. Even Joe never locked the front door physically, although he had kept it well locked emotionally. "Won't be a minute," Ted called to Mallard.

"No hurry, sir," said Mallard. They were back to the old relationship, employer and employee.

"I've left my car at your house," I said.

"So you have. Never mind, I'll drive it over later. I've got to see Dorothy Wigmore."

"Then *you'll* be stuck without a car."

"No," he said absently. "David Griffith will be there. He can give me a lift home. Look here, Selina, you ought not to leave your door unlocked when you're out."

"But I always do." I was surprised.

"I'm not sure if it's safe!"

"Oh, here in the valley, surely it's safe," I protested.

"Times have changed."

"But you never lock your door."

"It's different for me," he said irritably. "My house is never really empty. I have servants, I have dogs. Here you are completely alone."

The white cat appeared at the door and strolled towards us. "I have a cat," I said.

"I'd rather you locked your door in the future. Promise me you will?" He took my hand and gripped hard. "You're too trusting, Selina."

Oh, no, I'm not, I thought. I'm not trusting at all. Perhaps I don't trust you too much, Ted. "No one will be there," I said, and made a sort of promise I'd be more careful, and then I walked with him to the car, and watched him get in. Mallard was still sitting squarely in the back seat.

"You're an unpredictable girl," said Ted softly. "Sometimes you look at me as if you liked me and sometimes you quarrel with me."

He didn't look happy, and his mouth had a tight, controlled look to it. Finally, I said: "I don't remember quarreling with you lately."

"Don't you, by God?" He started the car savagely.

As he drove away I heard him say: "You don't remember much."

I wanted to run after him and bang on the car and shout: "Tell me what I don't remember then, tell me."

As if to prove Ted right and me wrong, Lizzie came forward from the kitchen, so there was someone in Catt's Tower. I suppose she'd been listening to every word.

"I've got someone to clean the house for you," she said, without preamble.

"Not you yourself?"

She ignored me. "Nice young married woman from the village. She'll come in every morning for a couple of hours."

"Well, thank you," I said doubtfully. "Who is she?"

"Sylvia Evans. Her husband works for Mr. Lestrange as cowman. They've only been married a few months and they haven't any children as yet. She's saving for a new bedroom suite, they're using his mother's at the moment, so Sylvy will be glad of the extra money."

"It's good of her." I knew how independent the village women were. It wasn't easy to get them to work for you.

"Sylvia says she can't rest easy in the bed. The old lady died in it, you know."

"Yes, I can see she might mind that."

"Oh, it's not the dying," said Lizzie briskly. "Sylvia's not the imaginative sort. She says it's dreadfully lumpy."

"Is Sylvia a short girl with dark curly hair and blue eyes?"

"Yes, that's her. She never uses a bit of make-up." Lizzie looked with faint disapproval at my own discreet eye shadow.

"I know her then. We were in the baby class at the village school together."

"So you were. That's nice, then."

"Lovely," I said, without enthusiasm. I remembered Sylvia clearly now. She had been a plump little girl with an ever-clean white starched pinafore and a stern conscience. The thought of having that sense of rectitude working in the house for me was not cheering.

"When's she coming?" I said, resigned.

"Probably she'll start next week. She's got to finish her week where she is. But she'll look in as soon as she can and give a hand."

"Oh, so she's got a job already?" I do remember being mildly astonished.

"Yes," said Lizzie and did not amplify it. "You can see me off now. Walk a bit down the path with me."

I went back into the house after she had gone and thought that perhaps it would be nice to have someone my own age around after all. I suppose I was missing Lynnet. The little white cat had joined me and Lizzie in the walk, and flitted ahead of me, making calling noises.

You can see that at that stage I wasn't putting two and two together. No, not at all.

When Lizzie had gone I locked the big front door and shut myself in with my white cat. If Lizzie was the old witch of Nun's Castle, perhaps I was the young witch. I felt like one, shut up here in my tower. The thought amused me. Certainly I had many of the attributes that, in the Middle Ages, might have won me the name of witch. I had the necessary book-learning, I had a cat, and I had a mystery about me. At one time, it would have been enough.

I woke up early next morning, and lay for a moment in bed wondering nervously how I felt. But I was normal. I passed a quiet, tranquil day, working.

Since the day was sunny and warm I took my lunch into the courtyard and ate sitting propped against a stretch of wall. The little cat came with me and played at catching flies.

Where I sat was within sight of the door of the dungeon. I was sleepy and my eyes closed. Dreaming there in the sun it was easy to imagine the castle as it must have been in its heyday, when the cobbles of the yard where I sat, now grass-covered, would have echoed to the sound of horses' hooves, and booted men. Where was now peace and quiet would then have been noise and bustle. There would have been the smell of cooking, the scent of baking bread, even the strong smell of beer brewing, for a medieval castle was a world complete in itself. It had to be, if it was to stand siege.

This castle had stood against more than one siege. Underneath where I sat was the mine or tunnel which the besiegers had tried to drive underneath the castle wall. They had got a good distance before they were stopped. Working from the outside as they did, they had had the advantage of heavier equipment than the defenders. The mine, accordingly, was wider and higher than the countermine that the besieged had driven in overhead, eventually opening up a hole in the roof of the mine from which to attack. I had knelt on the floor of the countermine once and peered through the hole and seen the mine below, just as the besieged must have done hundreds of years ago.

But while my imagination was absorbed in what was, to me, the pleasurable contemplation of an ancient war, I was deeply thoughtful.

I had begun to notice a repetitiveness in the events happening to me. Every so often my ownership of Nun's Castle would come into the conversation and the suggestion would be made that I sell it. I had made the suggestion myself, originally idly, casually to David Griffith. But then had come an offer on the telephone from an unknown buyer; this I had rejected. Ted Lestrange had made an offer to buy as well. I had refused this also. I did ask myself, cynically, whether Ted's anxiety to find Lynnet was not, somehow, connected with her co-ownership of the land.

I opened my eyes and took up a small notebook I used for writing odd things. I called it my commonplace book. I selected a clean page and wrote "Nun's Castle as Property" at the head.

It wasn't much of an observation, but it would do to begin with. I was beginning to have the idea that it would be a good thing if I used my mind on my life as it was at present, instead of reacting emotionally to each episode as it happened to me.

Underneath Nun's Castle, I wrote, "Lynnet ran away." I underlined the words. It seemed to me important that Lynnet had gone in this way. I got up and went back into the house. I took out the letter which Lynnet had addressed to me and never posted. I know I had blamed Joe for hindering its dispatch to me. Now I was no longer so sure. I was inclined to think that Lynnet herself had put it away in a drawer, unposted. I opened it again. So far I had read it only once and that in a cursory fashion. It had, in truth, been too painful to dwell upon. But I felt now I wanted to study it again.

The letter was as I remembered it: a short, untidily written and badly spelled letter, saying that she was desperate and wanted to get away and be alone. How strange, I thought, for Lynnet, who hated solitude, to be alone. I picked up the letter and studied the word again. Yes, it was "alone," she had written. Even blotched and smudged with water or tears it could be nothing else.

Then, for the first time, I saw that inside the envelope was a thin piece of paper. There were some lines on it written in Lynnet's hand and written carefully as if she was copying them.

> The rusted nails fell from the knots
> That held the pear to the garden wall.
> The broken sheds looked sad and strange.
> Uplifted was the clanking latch;

Weeded and worn the ancient thatch
Upon the lonely moated grange.
She only said: "My life is dreary."
"He cometh not," she said.
She said "I am aweary, aweary:
I would that I were dead."

I went back and sat in the sun and watched the clouds move across the sky and the colors change and fade in the trees across the valley as the light varied. A cold wind had sprung up and I shivered.

Lynnet had been unhappy, and not because she had quarreled with her brother Joe, although she probably had, but because she was in love and wretched and the man had rejected her. Joe is dead, I thought, but he didn't drive Lynnet away; someone else did.

There was a certain similarity between *my* predicament and Lynnet's, I thought wryly. Love and loneliness seemed to enter into it for us both. We both appeared to have a disappearing bridegroom.

I took my notebook out again and this time I wrote: My Demon Bridegroom.

A sick joke, I supposed, but it had an appeal for me at that moment as the sun began to go behind a cloud. It is a good folklore theme: the Demon who loved you and rides away, sometimes allowing you to remember him, sometimes effacing everything except a vague dream of bliss, but always leaving his bride with child. Cynical country tongues often put a grosser gloss on the process.

I felt my hands begin to sweat. In the city, I was a free, rational soul. At home in Nun's Castle, I became imaginative, vulnerable. I preferred to be rational, but I had truly cut myself in two and I had to learn to live with both parts.

I got up and went back into the house, waves of sickness passing over me. I had finished being sick, but was still feeling weak and cold, when the telephone rang.

The little cat began prancing around the telephone as I picked up the receiver. "Hello?"

"Miss Brewse?" The woman's voice was unknown to me.

"Yes." I pushed the little cat away and struggled to keep my voice steady.

"Dr. Timberlake's Clinic."

"Oh, yes," I said glumly. I could almost guess what was coming.

"Your report is negative." Her voice was absolutely level and virtually expressionless, training I suppose, because she must often find herself in a position where feelings must not be revealed.

I received the news in a silence that ran on unbroken for a moment. I remember stroking the cat. Then I became aware she was talking again.

"Dr. Timberlake wishes to speak to you. I will put you through."

His voice came through, serious and even sad. "Timberlake speaking. We have an arrangement to meet. Please do not break it. Or be late. I'll talk to you when I see you."

"Yes, I want to come," I said. "I need to talk to you."

I went into the courtyard after I had finished the telephone call. I wondered what the doctor was going to say to me. I felt no lifting of the spirits. There was something bad still to come; I was sure of it.

I rallied myself. I was not pregnant. I must approach the marriage certificate in a harder frame of mind. All my training had taught me how to handle documents. I must not be bullied by one.

The wind had dropped and the air was still. There stretched above me a bowl of pale blue which faded to white and then turned to a lemon yellow.

I remember thinking: what a marvelous *mad* sky.

Chapter Five

That night the long summer at last ended, the temperature dropped rapidly and everywhere there was snow.

In these valleys and hills snow still counts as a hazard, and I knew, as I opened the door and looked out, that the centuries had rolled back and it would be as hard now to communicate with the wild beyond Nun's Castle as in the fifteenth century. Today it was deep and treacherous.

The season was early for snow, but here in the hills it could happen, and, although in the valley it would soon melt, higher up it would pile up.

Nun's Castle had thick walls and was therefore much the same temperature inside, both summer and winter, cold, in short. Once I had hardly noticed this chill, but my years away from its rigors had softened me. Now I shivered. I ate my breakfast sitting close to an electric heater.

But the snow had brought me peace and privacy. I knew that for a few hours, at least, no one, not Lizzie Meredith, not her substitute, Sylvia Evans, not David nor Ted Lestrange would disturb me. The two men would be anxiously assessing the damage to their farm stock; the two women would be housebound. No true countrywoman would trudge through the snow to Nun's Castle. Even Lady Dorothy would not explode into my life, because she was away from home. Lizzie had brought news that M'Lady had flown to Paris for a visit to her cousin. Of course, she had a cousin in Paris and, lo and behold, this cousin had married a couturier and was always glad to see Dorothy and show her the latest collection. It was a puzzle why Lady Dorothy took this twice yearly trip; as her clothes were invariably the same classic English tweeds and jersey dresses, she always looked exactly herself. Joe used to say that Dorothy must have a lover in Paris, but I doubted this myself. I think she really went to buy clothes and did indeed buy clothes and even wear them, but that her strong personality reduced them all to a sort of background, so that whether she were wearing Dior or Givenchy they all became Lady Dorothy's style. This was my theory anyway, and just as likely as the lover.

As if to spite me, the telephone rang. Reluctantly I answered it.

"Are you all right?" asked Ted. "Got everything you want up there?"

"I could stand a siege," I said.

"I don't think it's that bad. But you won't try and get out today until the roads improve?"

"Probably not," I said cautiously, not revealing that I had every intention of driving to meet Dr. Timberlake. "I have plenty to do here."

"Hasn't Sylvia Evans come then?" he said incautiously.

So then I knew who had persuaded my old school friend Sylvia to come and work for me, and that she was just as much a bugging device as any Mr. Mallard had suggested. Sylvia was there to watch me. Or guard me. I didn't mind which you called it.

"No, Ted, she hasn't, and I'm not sure I shall want her if she does."

I cut his protesting voice off in mid-speech and went back to my cold cup of coffee and my colder kitchen.

I guessed now that Sylvia would be there eventually and that the snow would not keep her away for long. The other thing I remembered from her childhood, as well as her virtue, was her doggedness in pursuit of duty. If Ted had persuaded her to work for him and made it worth her while to do, then she would get here.

The nice idea, I thought maliciously, would be to be out when Sylvia Evans arrived.

And I had something I wanted to do if I could only contrive it. I wanted to make a study of the big wall painting in the chapel. Originally medieval, it had been restored by Dorothy's great-great-grandmother and touched up recently by Dorothy herself. I had been told there was a coat of arms still discernible in one corner and untouched up and unembellished, I hoped, by Lady Dorothy and her forebears. If I could see it clearly, it would help identify the patrons of the Abbey.

Before I could depart, Sylvia Evans had arrived. I heard the big front door open, and then I heard a stamping of feet to shake the snow from them, and then heard a knock hailing me. "Hello, there."

I knew it for Sylvia's voice at once. Voices are amazing.

The infant Sylvia had spoken in a ruminative, slightly reproachful voice, as if she suspected you of getting her into trouble, and the adult Sylvia faithfully reproduced the tone. I wondered briefly if her mother had spoken in this way and her mother before her and the voice had projected itself down the years. Did it make for a happy married life? I wondered.

I walked into the hall. Sylvia gave another little stamp with her feet and then stepped clear of the blobs of snow. "Hello, Selina."

"I didn't think you'd get here, Sylvia, on a day like this."

"Oh, I don't take notice of the weather," said Sylvia briskly. "I'm a good walker. It'd have to be pretty bad to stop me. Besides, I promised Mr. Lestrange." She stopped, suddenly.

"Yes, I know you did."

"I promised I wouldn't say." She looked at me with reproach: already, as she had suspected would happen, I had led her astray.

"I won't report you," I said, half-amused and half-cross.

She had not taken off her coat. "I can't stay. My husband's not well. 'Flu, I think. I don't like to leave him, you see."

"You shouldn't have come up all this way and tired yourself just to see me, Sylvia," I said at once.

"I *promised.* I'm not tired. I never get tired. My husband says I'm like a little pony."

I laughed; it was true, there *was* a likeness to a stocky Welsh cob.

"So there it is," said Sylvia. "I came, you see. But if

you're sure you're all right, then I'll go again and see you next week. He'll be better by then."

"If you're sure," I said doubtfully.

"Oh, they're a strong family, the Evanses, and never take anything bad. I ought to know, for I'm one myself. I married my cousin."

"Did you, Sylvia?"

She nodded with a pleased self-conscious flush rising on her cheeks. "It wouldn't do except with good health in the family. You've got to think of the children, haven't you? But we're all as sound as bells."

"Well, you go back and nurse him. I'm fine." I walked toward the door with her. "I'm going out myself soon."

"You are? Look after yourself then, Selina. Been ill yourself, haven't you?"

She was well informed and knew much more about me than I knew about her. "I'm better," I said. I watched her plod off down the road, happy and satisfied that she had done her duty. I looked up at the sky, assessing the weather.

It was cold enough . . .

It was cold enough to wear a fur coat, but mine, such as it was, remained in London. I knew Lynnet did not own one, but there was an aged beaver coat, almost threadbare, which had belonged to our great-aunt Minny Catchpole in the days of her youth. Aunt Minny had died, full of years, before we were born, but her coat lived on. This beaver coat was always worn by anyone who felt the need of it and could support its great weight. As children we had borrowed it for dressing up and keeping warm at bonfire parties and once it had spent a night on a snowman as his topcoat. I seem to remember we were trying to build an Abominable Snowman under Joe's direction, and Aunt Minny's coat formed his furry pelt. Those were the good days before things grew sour, and we all suffered what you might call a sharp attack of puberty.

I went to the cupboard where the coat used to be kept. I was not frightened that the coat would no longer be there. Not much was thrown away at Nun's Castle and possessions filtered up from generation to generation. This had its charm as well as its exasperations. Visitors often exclaimed with pleasure at being offered tea from an old Worcester Dr. Wall teapot, but were less pleased to find an ancient tiger skin complete with head decorating their bed to keep them warm.

There, hanging stiffly against the wall, was the coat, so old and so much used that it retained the shape of a plump human body, and so good in its day that it still looked falsely opulent.

I reached over to take the coat. I had to step into the crowded closet and lean over all the objects that were stored there. It was then I saw something pushed underneath a low shelf. I could hardly believe my eyes. It was the last thing I expected to see.

Abandoning the coat, I pulled the object out. It was light and presented no difficulty, but my astonishment and, yes, alarm, was sharp. What I had found was a wicker basket lined with quilted white cotton printed with red flowers. The basket was new. It didn't need close observation to see that no baby had ever slept in it, there was a sparkling newness about it that the first usage dulls.

I sat back on my heels and stared at it. I knew I had seen the identical basket in Bonwit Teller's in New York. And as if to reinforce the thought there were the remains of the big cardboard box in which it had traveled and on which was a torn label bearing their address. The addressee's name was gone.

I will own that my hand trembled as I restored the cradle to its position. There they were, the little red lions, bold and clear. And now I looked more carefully; they were indeed tiny little animals and not, as I had thought in New York, flowers. They were whimsically observed and drawn but recognizably lions.

I wondered what I had really seen in New York and when and for what reason my memory had gone wrong. Had I seen the lions and made a puny joke about dandelions and then remembered the joke as the reality? But if so, why? What was there about red lions my mind rejected? There was something at the back of my mind, and I fumbled for it. Somewhere, sometime I had a memory of a red lion. But I couldn't get it clear and I had to leave it.

Pulling on the big fur coat, I opened the door on to the courtyard. The little cat darted ahead of me, shaking her paws free of snow at intervals and then prancing on. I followed more slowly, placing my feet with care. I knew how easy it was to slip and fall. The cat left me when I stepped over a low wall and took a short cut down the slope of the castle mound to cross to the rising ground on which the chapel stood. There was a group of trees at the bottom with a stream running through them. I could see this grove, standing out clear and calm, against the snow.

I soon found the path. I knew it well. We had passed down it so often as children. Soon the ground sloped sharply as the path neared the clump of trees and I found myself breathlessly clutching at a holly shrub to stop my descent. The bush held me effectively and I stood there for a moment getting my breath back. The thorns had pricked my hand and a tiny bead of blood formed on my forefinger. I wrapped my handkerchief round my finger, and then moved down toward the river. It was cold under the trees out of the sun.

The stream was running clear and dark. Trout leaped there and little fish of nameless origin darted round the stones. I believe that centuries ago the river here had been broader and deeper but the dam which had been built higher up in the hills had changed the water level and tamed what must have once been turbulent waters.

I stood there for a moment, looking and remembering. I had never much liked the grove, it struck me as a place of ill omen; but we had played there often as children. I was staring down into the shadowed water when I heard the bell.

I lifted my head and listened. The sound was very clear and very precise, as if the cold air had accentuated those qualities. The bell was ringing slowly, one, two, three. I knew what the bell was, of course: it was the bell of the chapel. And as I stood there listening, I thought it sounded ominous. I stood there in the still air and listened to the bell and it rang like a knell.

There was a ford across the stream just beyond an elm. I suppose there had been a ford here at this spot since men first walked the track, which itself went, I am sure, back beyond recorded history. I always believed it to be a bronze-age pathway used by the early settlers.

The stepping stones were frosty beneath my foot, but I stepped carefully across the stream, passed through the belt of trees on the other side and began to labor up the hill, pulled down by my heavy fur coat.

Halfway up the hill I paused for breath, still listening to the bell delicately tolling.

"Never send to know for whom the bell tolls; it tolls for thee." These famous, often-quoted words floated irresistibly into my mind, words which carry a sort of romance with them now, but which to Donne, who had heard the plague carts rumble and creak, had a bitter hard meaning. I too felt the whip of the words and became, unaccountably, frightened of the bell. Why should they be making this solemn noise on this autumn morning? What did it portend?

I scrambled up the last steep yards of the hill to where the ground leveled out to approach the chapel. On my left hand was the gravel path which led to Marchers, the small but elegant stone house lived in by Lady Dorothy. This was my favorite view of her house. The present house had been built in 1740, but a house had stood on the site for six hundred years at least before that date. I could see the house easily from where I stood, and I knew that behind its plain well-bred face lay warmth and sumptuousness that its original builders had never dreamed of housing. I was fond of the house, but I thought always it had a secretive, bland look, and now with the shutters closed it looked dead.

The bell had stopped ringing as I approached the chapel. I assumed that the bellringer had seen me coming.

I pushed the big door open and stepped inside. It was a beautiful chapel, and I loved it, but it held for me no particular feeling of sanctity, although I suppose it should have. I guessed its long years as a ruin, before Lady Dorothy's great-great-grandmother had restored it, had taken some essential spirit from it. And yet, it had an atmosphere of its own. I stood there for a moment, assessing it. Mixed emotions seemed to rise within me. The place had the air of being greatly treasured, greatly loved. If this was not a place of worship it was yet a place for reverence.

I took a step forward. "This is an honored place," I said, half-aloud.

"They've taken the flags away," said a voice from the entrance to the bell tower.

I turned round to see a small man standing in the shadow of a pillar. He was wearing a thick countryman's suit and heavy boots. He looked a gentle soul, his face thin and scarred with age. This must be Old Harry.

"Flags?"

"Banners more properly speaking," he said, with an inward-looking smile at the memory of the glories of those banners. "Full of strange devices, all colors and gold."

"Oh yes," I nodded. No doubt Lady Dorothy had decorated the chapel for some fresh purpose of her own. She was always up to something here.

"I was sorry to see them go, things of beauty they were. Well, I must get back." His face—a most expressive, wrinkled face—became sad. He turned round and walked back into the bell tower. I saw him reach for the bell rope. I thought we'd had enough of the bell, even if he did enjoy it.

"Why are you ringing the bell?"

"For her. I'm tolling the bell for her."

"For whom?"

"Her that be dead." He looked at me wisely. "She don't know that she be dead and she's still walking."

I stared at him. He seemed so quiet and gentle and sincere. He believed what he was saying. David had said he was old and simple, not that he was crazy.

"Where does she walk?" I said.

"Why where she lived, of course," he said simply. "Haven't you seen her, then?"

"No." I could feel my heart banging. I wasn't

frightened of him as a person, but without effort he was summoning up a terrifying picture of a woman walking restlessly about where she had lived, unable to give herself up to death. It fed the imagination. "I haven't seen anyone."

"You don't always see her." He spoke with the air of one imparting a secret. "Sometimes it's just her voice, sometimes just the feeling that she has been there."

"Why do you ring the bell then?"

"To help her settle," he said simply. "She must rest in the end." He dropped his bell rope and came over and stared me in the face. "Who are you?" he said gently. *"Who are you?"*

For a moment I did not realize what he meant, then the chilling implication came through to me. "I'm Selina Brewse," I said sturdily. "Selina Brewse. And I'm not a ghost."

"I've often wondered if she knows," he said, still with that chilling simplicity.

"Well, I do," I said sharply. "Feel me and see," and I held out my arm.

He did, too, and gave me a sharp pinch with his tough old countryman's fingers. Then the ridiculous side of it all, how I was letting myself be pinched by a mad old bellringer to prove that I wasn't a ghost struck me, and I wanted to giggle. But I restrained myself in deference to his gravity. "Beg pardon, miss. I hope I haven't hurt you."

"No matter." I rubbed my arm. "I asked you to do it. I don't blame you for doing it properly."

"It's always best to make sure. Well, I'll just get back to my bell." He turned away. "A few more pulls." He hardly looked up to it, he was so frail.

"Wait." I put my hand gently on his arm to hold him

back. "Don't you think you've tried hard enough today? She'd want you to rest."

"Do you think so?" He sounded uncertain, as if he longed to rest, but knew he must soldier on.

"I'm sure of it." I dropped my hand. "You go on home. I'll stay here. And before I go I'll give the bell three last pulls for you."

He buttoned his coat and pulled his woollen scarf more closely round his neck. "I'll just be getting off home then." He shuffled off toward the door, and there he paused for a moment, and then turned round and said: "Don't do anything you don't believe in, miss." He was earnest.

"No, I won't," I promised. "When I ring the bell I shall believe in what I do." I told myself that I could believe in anything for the time it took to ring the bell three times.

When he had gone, closing the door quietly behind him and pointing out where the key to the big door hung, I walked through the narrow band of sunlight down the center of the church to study the mural, which lay in shadow. The colors came across better in the shade; I thought Lady Dorothy had done a remarkably good job of restoring the paintwork. Her color sense was more sophisticated than I would have expected, but she was constantly surprising me. I thought she'd improved it indeed, since her great-great-grandmother's day, otherwise the picture was as I remembered it. The saint to whom the chapel was dedicated, thought to be St. Clare, stood smiling in the center, her hands clasped on her slightly prominent stomach. Behind her, becomingly grouped, stood the donors of the chapel: two men and a woman, all three richly dressed and wearing golden ornaments. The woman, who wore a diadem of gold set with colored stones, held out a wooden casket to the saint. The casket presumably represented or even contained the donation. It was the sort of group you must have seen in many a medieval Flemish or Italian painting.

The two men had wooden, stiff features, but the lady was more successful as a portrait. She gazed out from under her stiff head style, her large blue eyes and fair skin matched by the reddish ginger of her hair. She had a certain hard charm.

There, in one corner of the picture, near to the right foot of one of the men was a heraldic shield. I couldn't make it out quite clearly, but unmistakably, and without question, there were four lions and three leopards. I looked again. The Plantagenet leopard for England and the red lions of Wales.

I made a note of what I had seen, thinking it was a memorable coat of arms which contained the signs of two royal houses, and this made me wonder why it had never been identified before.

There was an easy answer to this one, of course, that it had been indecipherable and Lady Dorothy, the romantic, had decided to do a good improving job on it. If you are going to touch up a coat of arms you might as well make it illustrious.

I repressed all comment in my own mind on the intrusive red lions. I dismissed them. Before I went I fulfilled my promise to Old Harry and rang the bell three times.

It was harder going home than coming. I was tired, to begin with, and beginning to worry about Lynnet again. So many things around me reminded me of her. Even the business with the bell stirred up memories. Not that we had gone in for bell-ringing, but the chapel had formed a part of our lives.

Lynnet had run away, hidden herself, because she was

unhappily in love. I was convinced of it. I could see that Ted thought she was dead, and although I could understand the reasoning behind this view, I didn't want to believe it. I wasn't sure I *did* believe it. The Lynnet I remembered had a good deal of bounce and would not easily give up.

Besides, she had telephoned me. I was convinced she had, and I thought she would telephone me again. In spite of what David had said about her malice and surreptitious unkindness about me, I believed she trusted me. If she was in real trouble and knew where to reach me, then she would try to do so.

Then I stopped. How had Lynnet known I was at Nun's Castle? She had telephoned me there. For the first time I realized that Lynnet might not be far away. She might be close at hand, watching and waiting.

Oh, silly Lynnet, I thought, why don't you hurry home?

Full of these thoughts I was walking faster and faster, in spite of the weight of the coat. I had reached the crest of the hill by the castle courtyard with a rush. Snow was falling again in lazy fat flakes, not heavily yet but promising more to come.

I walked across the courtyard and round to the front. It was then I saw the footprints. They came up the wide short drive to the house and showed up clearly in the snow.

So I had had a visitor. Someone who must still be there. The footprints led up to the door, but not away. I found my heart beating hard. Ted Lestrange and David Griffith would have driven to the door. Lynnet might have walked.

I hurried to the door, hoping either to find my visitor, hoping, believing, that it must be Lynnet. The great door stood open, the glass inner door was never locked, anyone could go in.

But hall, living room and kitchen were empty. I glanced hurriedly in each and saw no one. Only a small pool of rapidly melting snow in the hall by the big oak chest showed me that someone had come in from outside and paused here for a moment.

For the first time I felt frightened. Ted had warned me to be careful and because I had seen no good reason to heed him I had taken no notice.

Pretending to be braver than I was, I went up the staircase. It was when you went up this staircase, narrow and irregular, that you remembered most strongly that Nun's Castle was built for war. The steps, now carpeted, once bleak stone, ran up the side of the tower and the staircase was pierced at intervals by small high windows. On four levels doors opened off to bedrooms and closets. Facing them, small doors opened into what had been garderobes or the present privies. We had bathrooms and running water on the other side of the tower now and the garderobes had become purely decorative cupboards, with the exception that on the very top level the garderobe did not exist, but instead a wide slit ran across the stone floor, the sides sloping inward sharply. Without doubt it was part of the drainage system. If you looked down the slit you could see, or so we always said as children, right down to the bowels of the earth. Certainly there was a big drop into the depths of the castle foundations and cold air came up. The place haunted my childhood and I was glad when at some time it was floored and the place turned over into a prosaic closet. Lynnet used it for her clothes, which she spread out lovingly. Because of the difficult and intractable nature of the stone surround, the floor rested on it like a lid. It didn't worry Lynnet, who tripped over the floor lightly and gaily.

I walked slowly up the stairs, looked in what had been Joe's bedroom, entered my own bedroom, and then went into the one upstairs. All were empty. Very slowly, I walked down the narrow steps.

Halfway down, my head came level with one of the window slits. I could see to the courtyard and observe the curving path leading to the front door.

Where there had been one set of prints I could now make out two. The newer prints led away from the front. While I had searched the house, my visitor had quietly crept away.

I almost fell down the stairs and rushed out onto the path and then out to the gate which led to the steep lane down to the village. But it was no good. On every side there was emptiness and, though I called, only silence answered me.

I went back into the house, locked the front door and opened the cupboard door to hang up my coat.

Then I saw that the door was not securely latched, as I had left it, but slightly ajar, and on the floor in front of it was a pool of water. Even as I watched the door moved slowly open.

It was the little white cat that was pushing through the door and for a moment I wanted to giggle. It was a classic moment of alarm, seen by me in many old films. Usually Bob Hope was there by the door, too.

But then I remembered that I had indeed latched the door and I stopped laughing.

Moreover, the little cat was carrying something in its mouth. It was a tiny circlet of colored balls which made a pleasant rattling noise as she dragged them across the floor. I saw it was nothing but a baby's toy. I looked from the toy to the direction from which the cat had come.

There, sitting in the gaily decorated basket, which had been dragged forward to a comfortable spot on the floor, was a blue-eyed baby with red cheeks and a crest of gold hair. For a child of so few months he had a formidable and forbidding expression.

"Hello," I said cautiously, more to cover up my own surprise and alarm than because I really wanted to greet him. I thought if I just stared and did not say anything he might yell. At the time I did not know him as I did later.

He continued his baleful, blue stare. I supposed he was a boy; already he looked masculine. I rather hoped not to have to find out; knowledge of this sort suggested an intimacy I would prefer to avoid. "We'd better discover where your mother is, hadn't we?" I said. I dragged his basket out into the room. "Funny thing, finding you," I said aloud. "What is your name, Moses?"

The little cat pranced into view again, this time without the rattle, having abandoned it somewhere, and now the baby did react. He opened his eyes even wider and stretched hopeful grasping hands toward the animal. But the cat, although young, was too clever to come within reach of those powerful fingers and sat down, well out of reach.

The baby opened its mouth and roared. "Shut up," I said, at once. To my surprise he did so. I bore the reaction in mind for future use, although I hoped our acquaintance would not continue too long. Quite honestly, he terrified me. I picked up the whole outfit, basket and baby, in my arms and staggered into the living room where I put them all down by the fire. He was astonishingly heavy, astonishing to me, anyway, unused to babies and accustomed to the light bones of the little cat.

I went to the window and looked out to see a veil of snow hanging outside the window. I knew what it meant from experience: the road down to the village would be blocked in a short time. I looked at the baby. He seemed quite peaceful but I did not fancy trying to take him through this snow to the village, and if I didn't act soon it would be impossible for anyone from the village to drive up.

I left him by the fire and went to the telephone. Underneath the table on which it rested I could see where the little cat had deposited the baby's toy. It was a pretty object; someone had chosen it with care and affection. The detached feeling I had about this baby broke up a little, and I began to see him as a person, the center of a network of relationships, and the focus of love and concern. I stared at him and he stared back, quite without fear. Whatever else, he was a courageous little customer. Now it seemed to me there was something very familiar about his features. He reminded me of someone I had seen. I left the telephone and took the toy over and dropped it into the basket. Then I knelt down and studied the small face.

"Are you Lynnet's child?" I said softly to him and held his warm hand in my own for a moment and studied it; you can often recognize inheritance in hands, and Lynnet had lovely hands, long and fine with almond-shaped nails. But I could recognize nothing; here were baby hands, pink and plump with nails like little spades.

When I went to the telephone it was to discover that it was out of order, and that baby and cat and I were shut up in Catt's Tower together, cut off from the rest of the world.

Ours is not an automatic telephone exchange. We still have our own operator and her cheerful voice is part of life in the valley. Collecting information and passing it on is her great interest in life and I knew she would be as cross at her enforced silence as I was at her deafness. In my experience these telephone cuts never lasted long. I looked forward to hearing Joan's cheerful voice very soon, because apart from anything else she was a great source of practical advice. I knew I could say to her: Joan, there's this baby left on me, what do I do? And she would say: Oh, my goodness, try the police. Or else, I should try the Cottage Hospital, dear, the Health Visitor is there today and she's sure to know what to do.

I walked back to the fire and sat down to stare into its bright red heart. I threw on another log and handful of twigs which blazed into a clear yellow light. I think I may have slept a little. I know I came to myself with a sense of time having passed. In spite of the fire I felt cold.

One thing seemed clear, none of us would starve, shut up in out turret. I had plenty of food in store and I had already discovered that, tucked in with the baby, and partly accounting for the weight of the basket, was a supply of food for him in tins and packets. It seemed he was partial to sieved apples and beef stew put in glass jars. I hoped whoever had provided these jars had judged his taste accurately; this baby didn't look the sort to argue with lightly, especially over his diet.

He was very quiet now and as I looked at him I saw he was asleep and the cat, too, neatly curled up in a ball of white. Idly, for want of something better to do, I switched on the radio. It was a program of music, gentle sweet tunes, out of keeping with the mood I found myself in. I suppose that all over the countryside housewives were going about their work, listening with pleasure as they did so. They worked, I sat idle, but I was cut off from them by more than my hands lying slack in my lap. I was living in a stranger, harsher world. Suddenly I realized I was listening to the song that Lynnet had sung. This time it was being played by a trio of piano, violin and cello. Lynnet had given it more heart. There were tears in my eyes, and rolling down my face before I could stop them. I was crying for everyone—Joe, Lynnet, myself, even a little for the baby. Say what you like, the baby was lost. He deserved a tear or two.

Then I got up and made myself a strong cup of hot tea and took it back to the fire to drink. The radio was playing all the time, unheeded. I was conscious of it only as a background.

So it was that the news bulletin was halfway over before I noticed it had begun.

We have a local radio station which gives us all our local news (we don't have much; usually farm prices make the headlines) as well as transmitting the main news from the national network.

The announcer was in the middle of a piece of local news when I started to listen.

The body of a middle-aged man had been found dead in his car on the outskirts of Hereford.

I won't say it didn't seem important, death is always important, but it didn't seem important to *me*.

Then, so unexpectedly that I jumped, the telephone rang. The voice was unexpected. It was a woman's. She started speaking without preamble.

"You have an appointment with Dr. Timberlake?" I suppose I made a sort of affirmative noise, I don't remember clearly, but she swept on. "Don't expect to keep it. He's dead."

"Dead?" I said, thinking of the slender, gentle man I had known.

"Yes, dead. And you know more about it than you should, don't you?"

"What do you mean?" I said sharply.

But there was no answer, the line was dead again, and although I tried repeatedly to get the operator, I got no answer.

But as I put the receiver down, I wondered, indeed, if that had not been the end of the conversation, and if my caller had said all she meant to say. She hadn't given her name or identified herself in any way, but I was in little doubt who it was.

From the voice my mystery caller was the woman nurse who had originally spoken to me when I called Dr. Timberlake.

She hadn't liked me then, she seemed to hate me now. Slowly I was taking in the implications of what she had told me. Dr. Timberlake was dead. I didn't know how he had died, although I couldn't help remembering the news item about the man found dead in his car.

One thing was certain, Dr. Timberlake had died unexpectedly, and I was accused of "knowing more about it than I should." There was an ominous ring to the phrase that frightened me.

I was frightened. The mysteries around were not clearing themselves up, as I had hoped, but were taking on a new shape and form. Death and violence were creeping in.

Nothing violent had happened close to me yet, but it was coming nearer. As I sat there, looking into the fire, I could feel it breathing over my shoulder. I was warm, and yet cold at the same time, an unpleasant state.

I walked over to the telephone and tried, once again, to see if the operator would answer. Somehow I knew there would be dead silence and there was.

I went back to the fire and threw on a log, sending up a burst of tiny sparks and then a leaping flame.

The baby woke up then, and, although he did not cry (he seemed well trained in that respect), he looked at me with an alert, intelligent gaze. I had seen that look on the face of the cat too often not to know what it meant. He was saying: I expect to be fed. The white cat stirred and stretched. She too was getting hungry.

I went into the kitchen and selected my favorite cooking utensil: a can opener. Joe had various frozen foods in the freezer, but an investigation had convinced me these were all of too exotic a nature to suit me, baby and the cat. The baby, as a matter of fact, would have his own tin of apple custard and I hoped he would enjoy it. Puss and I could share a tin of beef stew and noodles. I carried the baby's basket into the kitchen and put him on the table where he could watch me. He did so, still with that attentive, silent face. The cat was talking for them both in a series of soft, rapid miaows.

I fed the baby first. I judged him to be over six months old, probably nearer nine months, but I was so inexperienced it might be wrong. It puzzled me, however, that he was so silent and immobile. I thought babies were active and restless. He was the least restless little creature I had ever seen. But he did not look stupid. On the contrary there was a look of perception, sharpness even, in those large eyes.

I'm not particularly fond of small babies; no one with

my particular upbringing could be. (We were bullied and chivvied into the adult world by the elderly aunt who brought us all up, and were taught to regard infantility as a crime to be lived through.) But I found myself touched by the fortitude and lack of fear with which he faced a stranger. He was a most unusual child.

After we had all eaten I sat there staring into the heart of the fire. There comes a time at all moments of crisis when a picture forms in your mind, whether you like it or not.

I began to see a picture of two girls, their lives intertwined, related through blood and affection. Two girls, of almost the same age, dissimilar in appearance, in spite of the blood tie, but similar in destiny. Two girls, both, for reasons I could not guess, under threat. Lynnet had run away. It might be best for me to do the same.

I looked at the baby: I was now chained to Nun's Castle by a stranger. For a wild moment I wondered if he had been left here for precisely that reason, but then I dismissed the idea.

I jumped up and ran to the telephone, and this time, in the mad way such things happen, I got the operator at once. She answered brightly, "Hello, how are you up there?"

I drew my breath in with relief. "I'm all right. What's been wrong with the telephone?"

"If I could shrug over the telephone, dear, I would. You know what we're like here. We'll have it fixed for the next bad weather, they say. Say it every time." She laughed. "They'll get round to it in their own slow time. I'll be dead first, I said last snow. How are you, dear? I've seen you driving around."

"I've got a baby here," I said abruptly. "I came back and found it here. What do I do?"

She made a sort of clucking noise. "Oh, dear, not another one? I thought that was all done with."

"You mean there have been others?"

"We've had a spate of it, dear. About half a dozen babies I should say. Picked up from one place and dumped down elsewhere on some stranger. Of course, they never came to any harm and soon got taken home again. I thought they'd got the girl who was doing it."

"Girl?"

"Yes, it was a hysterical trick. She wasn't quite right, poor thing. She'd lost a baby or something. But I was told they'd got the girl . . . These things do get copied, though." She went on uneasily: "You get another silly kid thinking it's a giggle. I'll tell the police for you. They can send a car up."

"Yes, do that."

"I suppose it's too young to be worried?"

"It's not worried," I said, looking at him.

"The usual pattern, none of the kids acted alarmed. Too young, I suppose. Some of the mothers minded the fact that the baby didn't care as much as they minded losing it! What is it like?"

"Reddish hair, big blue eyes, pink cheeks. Good-looking child, really."

"Could be anyone, couldn't it? No, I don't know it. Boy or girl? You did not say."

I hadn't said, she was quite right. It was odd. Was it because, in some obscure way, I felt his sex to be important? "It's a boy."

"Well, of course, if I *hear* of anyone having lost him I'll ring you straightaway."

"Provided you can get through."

"There's always that, isn't there?" she said, game to the last.

The line was broken again before I realized I had not asked her about Dr. Timberlake. But if my mind had blocked this question, the talk with her had cleared something else. As if a channel in my mind had cleared itself and was now running smooth and strong, I realized that I knew the child.

I turned to him. "Boy," I said, "I've seen you before. You were christened in the chapel and I saw you there."

It was fantastic that I should have forgotten or failed to remind myself of the resemblance. I had had only one glimpse of the baby at the ceremony, but now I was absolutely sure of the identification.

Light was pouring in on me now. I knew more than I thought. "I remember who you remind me of," I said to the child. "You are like the Princess in the wall painting. You have a look of her."

The human mind is very strange. For a little while, after I had said this aloud, I felt gay and relieved as if I had solved all my problems. I tidied the baby up (in this respect, as all others, he treated me in a most civilized fashion) and set the basket back by the fire.

The day was drawing in and, although it was still early, the room was dusky. I began to turn on lights. My hand was actually on a switch when another door opened in my mind and I sat down heavily.

I remembered the little red lions on the lining of the baby's basket where he was so peacefully asleep. I remembered that the basket had been sent from New York. I remembered the four red heraldic lions in the wall picture.

I knew then that this child had not been placed in this

house by chance. Never mind if there had been a pattern of baby-lifting already. Never mind if that had been the source of the idea. This baby was not part of that pattern.

I thought of the careful way in which the basket had been packed with a toy and some food. The child had been placed in this house deliberately. I knew that, in some manner which I did not understand, I had brought him here.

I leaned forward. "Have you come to stay?" I whispered softly. The child did not move his head. I clapped my hands smartly. He still did not move. The child was deaf.

Suddenly, I was once more in touch with the outside world: the telephone rang. I leapt to answer it.

"Hello," said Joan's cheerful voice. "I thought I'd tell you that I'm having difficulty reaching the police station."

"I'm not surprised."

"No, it's not the weather, there's trouble of some sort and it's all hands to the deck." Joan liked a nautical allusion occasionally. "The station Sergeant's wife is taking messages and she says she'll pass the word on about the baby as soon as she can, but don't expect much help today."

"Did she know anything?" I asked, but it was too late, Joan was gone again. I didn't try to ring her back. I knew her powers of magically disappearing.

It was later than I expected when I looked at my watch. The day seemed to have disappeared in the strangest way. The morning, when I had heard the chapel bell tolling and had talked to the old man, seemed both very close and very far away.

But I took a decisive step.

I walked upstairs, opened my case, took out an envelope and, breaking the seal I had placed on it, removed the document it contained and carried it downstairs.

Then I put on my spectacles, which I only needed on really serious occasions, spread the copy of the certificate of marriage on the table, and studied it sensibly. I use the word sensible and this is what I was. I put all my own emotions on one side and studied the photocopy in an objective manner.

At once I saw what I should have seen before. It was a fake. A fraud. A cheat.

An arrant forgery, put together like a bad piece of sewing, and I ought to have known better than to be deceived for a moment.

In the part of the document where my name was written slight shading was visible, and the ink looked darker. At first I had assumed this to be a trick of the photograph. But as I looked at it now I was convinced it was because the text had been doctored; one name had been erased and my name put in its place.

At this point I felt a wonderful surge of confidence, as if my feet were on solid ground at last. I was so happy it was unbelievable. I hummed to myself as I returned the "certificate" and locked it carefully in the drawer. I did not know yet what action I would take, although finding the actual document and verifying my suspicions must come soon. I wasn't exactly sure how to lay my hands on the original, but as an historian I knew that there was more than one way of checking on the accuracy of a document. I felt confident I would know how to handle it; all my training had taught me what to do. Thank goodness, I thought, this is something real, at last.

I felt quite joyful as I attended the baby and fed the cat. I washed my hair, always a sign of renewal with me, and I was sitting by the fire drying it, my cheeks flushed and warm with the heat of the fire when, for the fourth time that day, the telephone rang.

I went slowly to the telephone this time. I did not want anything to challenge my state of euphoria. Still, it had to be answered.

I heard the urgent, deep tones without surprise. Somehow I knew it would be him. "Selina? I've been trying to telephone you for some time," said Ted Lestrange.

"I think the line has something wrong with it. Unless Joan's doing it on purpose," I said slowly. "I have considered the idea."

"I don't know what you're talking about," he said irritably. There was that special note in his voice I was hearing lately.

"Never mind."

"I'd better come right out and say what I have to say, Selina. You've been seeing Dr. Timberlake, haven't you?"

"I saw him once." My voice was cold.

"You were to see him today?"

"Yes. I don't know how you know. Did I tell you?" I knew I had not.

"I know without your telling me. I've known you were worried and upset about something." He sounded unhappy. "You know he is dead?"

"Yes. I heard it on the radio. And you aren't the first person to telephone me about it. But the first person was anonymous," I said, unable to keep the asperity out of my voice. "I think I know who she was, though."

"Tell me about this, Selina."

I gave him an account of my brief but unpleasant telephone call. He listened without saying anything. Then: "I'm afraid you must have an enemy there. That explains a lot. Listen, Selina, I've been talking to the police. Dr. Timberlake was found dead in his car. He was shot, once, in the head. He was slumped across the driving wheel."

As if from a very long way off I heard myself saying: "Did he kill himself?"

"No. Selina, are you listening?"

"I'm listening."

"The car was parked in a side road, as if he had drawn up there to talk to someone he knew. The police think it was murder. It seems he left his surgery early this afternoon and cancelled all his appointments. He told his secretary he had to meet someone. She thinks it was a woman."

I absorbed this information silently, wondering why the doctor's secretary had assumed, as I now supposed she had, that this woman was me. Then I became aware of what Ted was saying.

"Of course, you are all right," he was saying, his voice urgent, "because you had Sylvia Evans with you."

I broke into his speech. "I know you sent her here. I had guessed she was your agent. Or spy." I was coldly angry. "But she had to go home because her husband is ill. Sorry, Ted."

This time it was I that broke the call. I put the receiver down hard. I thought I heard his voice say, "Darling, oh darling."

I knew I had not been out of Nun's Castle since that morning. I knew I had not met Dr. Timberlake that day. I knew I had not shot and killed him. But it might be hard to prove.

Silently my brief happiness had faded. I carried the

baby in his basket up to my room and prepared to go to bed, if not to sleep. The cat followed us up, then leaped on my bed and sat down to watch me prepare.

I undressed and put on a thick quilted dressing gown of red silk. Then I sat down in front of my dressing table to clean my face. I stretched out my hand for the tub of cleansing cream. Suddenly I gave an involuntary scream and jerked my hand away.

My finger had touched something penetrating and sharp. I drew the cream closer and stirred it with a nail file. The cream was filled with razor sharp slivers of glass. If I had slathered it on my face, in the way I normally did, my face would have been cut as if by a razor.

I threw the pot into the wastebasket at my feet. But as I did, I realized that only someone who knew me and my habits intimately could have planted the glass. I felt sick.

I went to the window, threw it open, and drew in some deep gulps of clean, sweet air. High above, the stars shone in cold silence. I wondered then if Lynnet was far, far away and if the same malignant juggler was playing a game with us both. Or if, on the contrary, Lynnet was terribly, terribly close.

At that moment I admitted to myself what, I suppose, any fool could have told me. I was on the brink of falling in love with Ted Lestrange.

But my deepest thoughts were all of Lynnet.

Chapter Six

It was the child that brought me out of my state of withdrawal and back to the world. After a day in which it had hardly opened its mouth, it woke up and started to cry. Cry is an understatement; bawl or roar was more like it. Starting in a small kind of way it worked up to great tearing sobs. I was very conscious of my ignorance. I picked the child up and nursed him, only to have his body go rigid in my arms. I took him to the window to stare at the moon and certainly for a second or two the pale radiance which filled the sky checked the screams, and he gazed in silence. Then he began with undiminished vigor. At the end of twenty minutes I was both terrified and exhausted. I began to wonder if he were seriously ill. I tried to telephone Joan, but, not to my surprise, the line was dead again. It was very difficult always to rouse our exchange at night. When I put the receiver down, my hand was trembling.

Then I noticed that the child had stopped crying and was watching me. He didn't look in the least ill, more baffled and cross. I felt the same way myself. Our eyes met and the message got through. "Why, I believe you are hungry!" I said aloud. How stupid I had been not to think of it before.

He started to sob again, long, almost musical sobs which widened his mouth, while his eyes kept a sharp watch on me. I tucked him in his basket and carried him down the narrow staircase to the kitchen. The cat, till then apparently deep in sleep, woke up at once and came too.

I heated some milk, fed some to the baby and poured a saucer for the cat. Peace came back to our little community.

It was warm in the kitchen and comfortable, but instead of its making me feel drowsy I felt alert and restless. I knew I would never sleep. I made some coffee and some sandwiches and carried them through into the living room. I built up the fire and drew the big chair close. The cat and baby slumbered not far away in the kitchen. I was on edge, listening for every sound. Old houses are full of noises; where the aged, dry wood contracts and creaks, the solid structure of the house moves imperceptibly but audibly. Plaster rattled behind the wainscoting.

The coffee was good, but as I finished it I thought some brandy would have improved it. Then I remembered that Nun's Castle had a cellar. In one of the very few letters I'd had from Joe he had mentioned the repairs he was doing to the cellars and the small amount of wine he was laying down.

"I suppose they would have had pipes of wine and barrels of beer in the old days," he had written. And I remembered writing austerely back that a pipe of wine was usually an exchequer measurement and rarely an actual cask full of wine and never an actual pipe, and that, in any case, in a well-run medieval castle wine and beer would be kept in different cellars. I don't know what use the cellars were put to in the days of our childhood when Aunt Minny and later Aunt Beatrice ruled the house, but they were certainly not used for wine. A bottle of sherry in the sideboard was Aunt Beatie's idea of a rich supply.

Curiosity, as much as anything else, made me get up and investigate. After all, the cellars were a part of my inheritance. But I also badly wanted something other to think about than myself and my worries.

I pushed open the door leading to the cellars and switched on the light. This, in itself, was new. In the old days a candle in an old metal candlestick had been left at the head of the stairs together with some matches. It was one of our dares as children to go down to the cellars in the dark, count ten and then come back. I was always terrified of the dark and still am. There were supposed to be rats, but I never saw any. Now the staircase walls were whitewashed and the stairs were plainly carpeted. As you would expect, the cellars at Nun's Castle were very large. Beside the stairway ran a wide ramp, down which, I imagine, supplies were rolled. This, too, was now neatly whitewashed. I walked down, flicking on light switches as I went. I soon saw that Joe had not attempted to redecorate the whole of the great area that lay under the tower. The entire space had been swept and tidied but only one vaulted cavern had been whitewashed and laid with a bit of red carpet. On a single wall was a rack holding bottles. On the wall facing me was a plain screen and in front a table and a group of chairs. On a raised stand by an armchair stood a film projector.

For a moment I was surprised, and then I realized how

natural a hobby making films and showing them would be for Joe, who had always enjoyed photography. I knew that, although he hated showing himself to the world, he could manoeuver himself around expertly in his chair and specially equipped motor car. He could get out into the world enough to observe it and photograph it, if he wanted to. Apparently he had so wanted and as a result I was the part-owner of a projector and some films, one of which was in position this minute, ready to be run.

I went over to the racks of wine and saw that Joe had been discriminating about his drink. A little burgundy, some claret, a few bottles of hock and half a dozen of moselle. I saw a bottle of brandy, but my desire for it had already evaporated.

I sat down in the armchair, switched on the film projector and sat back to watch. I had already listened to Lynnet singing, as Joe had listened in the last few hours of his life. Now I would see something on which his eyes had focussed not long before he died. One way and another, I was getting very close to my cousin Joe. The focus of the lens needed a little correction, but it was a model with which I was familiar, having used one myself, and I was able to adjust it.

The picture moved into view. It was an amateurish beginning. A few people moving slowly in and out of the camera's eye against a background of trees. Then the film moved on and we were inside a building. I soon made out what it was all about. It was the film of a country wedding. Boring, I thought, and not very like Joe, who hadn't enjoyed weddings.

I took the bottle of brandy and went back upstairs and

drank a little with some coffee. The brandy didn't taste of much and neither did the coffee. I wasn't thinking of either. I was really summoning up strength of will to go back and study the film again.

I sat there for about half an hour, then I took my spectacles (which I hardly ever wore) and went downstairs for another look at the film. It was long past midnight but I was no longer tired.

I ran the film through again, and this time I seemed to get a clearer view. It ran for about eight minutes and some of this was made up of wasted shots of either blurred or obscure visions. The total viewing time was not great. What I saw was the record of a wedding in the country made by a beginner in film-making. In fact, I'd be surprised if the photographer had ever made one before. Because of this ineptness some of the things I wanted to see were tantalizingly difficult to make out. In addition, it was a color film, but either the film was wrong for the camera or else the cameraman had made some mistake, because all the colors were muted in tones of the mist, blue and gray, with here and there a hint of violet and a threat of red. In its way it was strangely beautiful, like a dream, but details retreated into the distance.

So there it was; I was watching the badly photographed film of a wedding. After a very few outside shots came the ceremony itself. I saw the bride walk up the aisle, I saw the bridegroom greet her. I saw the congregation, what there was of it, and I saw, distantly, a ceremonially attired figure come forward to commence the marriage ceremony. The eye of the camera had been turned toward the altar and therefore one saw more of the backs of the actors than their faces.

When, as occasionally happened, a face was turned toward the camera, the incompetence of the cameraman prevented recognition. It was maddening.

I soon realized where the scene was being filmed. It was in the Nun's Chapel itself. I could see the walls, the great windows and the vaulted ceiling.

After running the film through, I went upstairs again and sat looking into the fire. I did wish I could have seen the bride's face. I almost wished the baby would waken again to distract me, but child and cat slept peacefully on. They might figure in my dreams, but I did not walk in theirs. I found I had left one sandwich uneaten from the earlier pile, and I ate it now with some gusto. It seemed to put new life into me.

I went down again and looked at the film for a third time. I saw now that the flashes of red and gold were colored banners and streamers hanging from the wall. These must have been what old Harry had talked about. Perhaps he was here among the people briefly shown on the screen. I did not recognize him, but now, third time round, I was beginning to get short glimpses of features I knew. Surely that was Lady Dorothy turning away from the camera? I could just make out her beaky nose and it rather annoyed me. What was *she* doing there? I wished I could see the bride's face but her stiff archaic head-dress prevented me.

In fact, none of the dress was modern. All the figures I could see appeared to be wearing formal, antique clothes of an unidentifiable but vaguely medieval style. It looked as though what I was watching was a film of a function similar to those I had helped Lady Dorothy organize. It was probably one of her earlier efforts. I knew she had tried her hand at various exploratory projects before she sought my advice, just as I knew she now had in mind other, even more ambitious projects, such as another tournament.

Judging by what I could see, this affair was, like the film itself, an amateur performance. The actors had an underrehearsed air of stumbling through their parts.

I stopped the film and thought. Yes, that figure in the long-sleeved gown did have a look of Lady Dorothy, but I couldn't be sure. I suddenly felt very weary. It was like looking at things through a mist; images formed, wavered and disappeared.

I took a deep breath and started the film once again. I had now seen the short scenes three times and each time I had got a bit more detail out of it. The fourth time does it, I thought.

I sat watching the first few flashes of movement on the screen idly for a minute, waiting for the interior scenes which interested me more. Then I got a shock. I suppose, really, I had all the time been noticing more than I knew.

I realized I had exclaimed aloud. I stopped the film and looked hard. Yes, surely there, half-hidden in the shadow of a bush was a figure in a wheelchair. Joe.

I stared as hard as I could, but there comes a point when an image can offer no more. You have to make up your mind on the evidence offered. Was it or was it not Joe? And if it *was* he, then who had taken the film? And if Joe had not taken the film, then why was he running it and what interested him about it so much?

Why did it interest *me* so much, for that matter? And I found that question hard to answer as I finally left the cellar. I went to bed then and soon to sleep, but only to dream. If it is true that we dream of the last things we saw or thought about before we go to sleep, then it is not surprising that I dreamed of a wedding. Saw again in my dream the very wedding I had just seen on film. What was surprising, and I remembered feeling this even in my dream, was my place in the wedding.

I was at the head of the procession that walked up the aisle. I could not see the face of the bride because it was *my* face. I was the bride.

I could feel the rich stiffness of the gown I was wearing. My hand as it brushed the side told me it was damascene, a silk with a woven pattern. On my head was the burden of a stiff head-dress, my hands were clasped tightly in front of me. Now I was twisting a ring on my hand. It felt both monstrously heavy and tight, like a ring of lead.

The aisle of the chapel stretched before me endlessly until I saw clearly that it was now a tunnel and that I was far underground. The tunnel narrowed toward the end. I could see the end of the tunnel as a small circle, a ring of light. I remember screaming as I felt myself being propelled toward the narrow tunnel end where the sides would press upon me.

In my dream one part of me was screaming and another part was coldly withdrawn, commenting upon my predicament and remarking that it was fantastic.

"What an image," I thought, "a tunnel contracting into a tomb."

I knew that was wrong as soon as I had said it because someone tapped my shoulder.

"Wake up, dear," said Lizzie. "I've brought your breakfast."

I sat up and looked at her. She was standing there by my bed, holding a tray, and smiling. The room was filled with hard bright sunlight reflected from packed snow.

"How did you get here?"

"Walked." She tucked a shawl round my shoulders and put the tray on my knee. "I've made the coffee strong. Just how you like it."

"Yes, but why did you come?"

"To see you, dear, just like always."

"Yes, but why did *you* come and not Sylvia?"

"To see you, dear, just like always. Sylvia and I are sharing you between us. I like to keep an eye on you."

She smiled blandly. Lizzie could be very annoying sometimes when she played stupid.

"I thought the snow would have kept you home. It always used to."

She continued to smile. "You've been away a long time, dear, and things have changed. The roads are better, to begin with, and then the county cleans the roads better now than when you were little. They put chemicals down and that melts the snow, or stops it freezing or something. It's going to thaw today, anyway."

"The breakfast is good, Lizzie." I was surprised how hungry I was and how good the eggs and toast tasted.

"I'm glad to have a word of thanks. I wondered when you were going to say it. You always used to have nice manners." She went to the window and adjusted the curtain. "By the way, who's the little stranger downstairs?"

"Oh, Lord, the baby, I've forgotten him."

"I thought you might have done," said Lizzie dryly.

"How could I come up to bed and forget him?"

"You never were the motherly type. Where's he from? Not yours, I hope."

I told her and she listened silently, nodding her head at

intervals. "I'd heard about the baby-stealing," she said. "Like Joan, I thought it was all over. The sooner you get on to the police the better, my dear." She sounded troubled.

"Did you recognize him, Lizzie?"

She was evasive. "It's hard to be sure at that age, dear, isn't it? I mean unless you know a baby really well, they can look the same."

I kept silent. I knew you could never press Lizzie beyond a certain point. She went away, and after a little while I heard her talking on the telephone. She seemed to be gone a long time.

"Just enquiring," she said when she came back. "Joan says no one's lost a baby that she knows of." She tucked the blanket closer and fiddled with the quilt. "It's a love child, you'll find, and it's been left on you to draw attention to it."

I frowned. "Why me?"

She shrugged. "You'll have to answer that yourself, Selina. Something to do with this house, perhaps. Could be Joe's child."

"Lizzie! You don't mean it?"

"Why not?" She sounded exasperated. "He was a man. He was up to it."

"He doesn't remind me of Joe," I said obstinately.

"You think you'd know, do you? You've got to remember the mother counts for something."

I stared at her. "If you're trying to tell me something, Lizzie, I wish you'd come right out and say it."

"Can't say what I don't know, m'dear. I've shocked you about Joe, I can see, but the fact of the matter is you live in a bit of a dream, Selina, and need rousing. I'd say someone was trying to attract your attention. What to, I couldn't say."

She was sitting on the bed, talking to me, when we

heard the sound of a car. Our eyes met. Then Lizzie went to the window.

"Going away," she announced. "It must have come in quietly while we were talking."

"Did you leave the door unlocked, Lizzie?" I asked.

"Yes. And left a window open."

Without another word she went out, and I heard her walking heavily down the stairs. In a short while she was back. "The child's gone. Love child or not, your charge has left you."

As mysteriously as he had come, the child had been taken away.

"I think I knew he'd go like that, Lizzie," I said. "I'm glad you saw him, or I might think I'd invented the whole episode . . . I hope he's all right. I'd got rather attached to him."

Lizzie shrugged. "Those that left him, took him. You'll have to tell the police, Selina. It doesn't make it any better that he's gone. Put yourself in the clear."

"I will," I promised.

She looked at the sky. "The weather's breaking up, my dear. It'll rain soon, I daresay, and then peace will be over for you. Look after yourself. They'll all be in on you."

She was gone, her words, a hint of menace to come, hanging in the air. I wondered who, apart from Joan, she had spoken to on the telephone. It was certainly my impression she had made more than one call. I had always trusted Lizzie completely and I still did, but I found myself wondering now what other loyalties she had.

I dressed and went downstairs. The snow was melting

and the roads were clearing. I had the feeling that action would soon be demanded of me. It was strange to feel threatened and frightened without knowing where the threat was coming from, or what was behind it. But someone hated me in a direct, physical kind of way. The glass in the face cream showed me that. I didn't want to believe it was Lynnet but it was someone who had observed me sharply. I didn't know what I had done to earn this malice. I remembered David Griffith's words and wondered if they applied here too.

Dismissing fantasy, I had one very practical thing to do. I was going to make a check on the marriage certificate sent to me. I was going to St. Kenelm's Church to see who had got married there on June the fifth of this year.

First, I had to find St. Kenelm's Church. I had many routes to its discovery close to my hand. On my bookshelves was a two-volume county history. St. Kenelm's sounded like an old foundation; a description of it was almost certainly within this local history.

A whole chapter chronicled parishes and their churches. This part of the county had been one of the first to be converted to Christianity and some of the churches went back to the eighth or ninth century. (Paradoxically, parts of the county had also clung passionately to paganism, which proved, I suppose, that whatever gods it had, it believed in them.) St. Kenelm's, as I might have guessed from the name, had a very long history. St. Kenelm himself was a Mercian, trained in Rome, who had then been sent back to convert his fellow countrymen. One of his converts came to this part of the world and named a church after his leader. Or so the tradition went. The county history told me that the present church dated from the fifteenth century and had been "much restored."

The history also told me one other significant fact: St. Kenelm's was one of the parishes of Peterschurch. I knew what that meant: some benefactor in the nineteenth century had spent a great deal of money doing things to the fabric and glass of the church which would have been better left undone.

It's surprising what help a telephone directory can be. I still had to find out the exact location of St. Kenelm's in Peterschurch, which was, as its name might have told you, well endowed with ecclesiastical foundations. Churches don't have telephones but rectors and vicars do. Without difficulty I found what I wanted. St. Kenelm's Rectory, Benson Alley, Holy Springs, Peterschurch. I knew where it was now. Holy Springs was the oldest and poorest part of Peterschurch.

I fed the cat and dressed myself to go out. I locked all the doors, closed the window and was just going out to get my car when the telephone rang. I was standing just by it and I could see my image in the great gilt mirror in the hall. I looked pale and tense. The mirror was old and my image wavered. It seemed a fair representation of me in my present uncertain state of mind.

I picked up the receiver. I didn't have time to speak before I heard that soft, husky voice. "Hello."

"Lynnet," I said sharply.

"Yes, Selina." Her voice was thick, as if she had been crying.

"What are you playing at, Lynnet? You've got us all worried. We want you here. Come home."

"I'm coming," she said.

"When?" I was being aggressive and I knew it, but her dreamy, faraway voice was annoying me. I had a bone or two to pick with Lynnet when I did see her.

"Today, now. I'm at Hereford. I'm coming by bus to Peterschurch. Can you meet me there?"

"Yes. As it happens I'm going there anyway. Tell me when to meet you."

"In two hours. At the bus station. Give me two hours."

I thought I could give her more than two hours and I had the feeling, a slightly vindictive thought, that this time Lynnet could wait for me.

I walked out of the house, closing the big door firmly behind me. The air had a milder feel than the day before, but it was damp and very cold. The sun had disappeared behind a bank of low cloud. Underfoot the crisp snow had softened. I guessed that the roads would be covered in a thick gray slush.

The sound of a car being driven at high speed up the hill surprised me. Someone was coming to call on me. I stood there looking as a neat, dark-colored car came smoothly into view and stopped quickly. There was something about its quick powerful arrival that I disliked.

If you've never been called on in an official way by the police, then it takes a moment or two for you to absorb the fact. Once absorbed, it sinks into your consciousness like a stone, disturbing everything.

But they were very polite, and pretended, perhaps even meant, that they did not wish to delay. If I were going out, then I was going out. We would just have a little talk, and then I could be on my way.

They invited me to sit in the car and talk to them there, so I installed myself on the back seat and one of them sat next to me, and the other sat in the front seat and turned round to talk at me. There was a driver in uniform who neither looked nor spoke. I liked him best.

They told me they were talking to every woman who had had an appointment with Dr. Timberlake yesterday. They also told me, what I might have known for myself, that my name was in his diary for the last appointment of the day.

"He left in the early afternoon in a hurry. He told his nurse to cancel all other appointments, but he didn't mention you, as if . . ." He hesitated and waited for me to speak. He was a tall fair policeman called Lewis and I knew him by sight as one knew most people thereabouts. His daughter had been at school with me and Sylvia Evans. Then he had been a Detective Inspector. Now he was promoted to a higher rank. He had called himself Superintendent Harold Lewis. The other man looked a blood brother to Mallard, and I would not have been surprised to learn his name was Swan. But, in fact, no one ever told me his name.

"As if he was going to meet me," I finished for him. "He didn't, though. I haven't seen Dr. Timberlake since our first and only interview."

"We are interviewing everyone as a matter of routine," observed Harold Lewis. I wondered if he remembered me from his daughter's early days at school, but he gave no sign. "Several people saw Dr. Timberlake get into his car and drive off. We are looking for people who saw him later. You were here all day yesterday? You didn't go out?"

"I was out in the morning for a little while. After that I stayed in the house."

"You did not use your car?" I had already sensed he was unobtrusively studying my small car. I saw his eyes move to the unmistakable marks of a car's wheels across the rapidly thawing snow. "You had a visitor?"

"Yes." Without time to think about it or choose my words, I was precipitated into telling him the story of the baby's arrival and disappearance.

He listened without much expression on his face. "You say you reported this last night."

"I tried. I told the telephone operator." I was grateful I had done this, because it substantiated my story at a time when, as I was beginning to see, innocence in itself was no help. "She told me she had passed the story on to the local police station but they were too busy to do anything about it."

He didn't like that, and I saw his eyebrows draw together in a frown.

"And now the baby has gone?"

"Yes."

He grunted. I was more than ever glad that, not only had I spoken about it to Joan, but also Lizzie had been there that morning. What a mercy she had turned up. "Do you have a gun, Miss Brewse?" he said, changing the subject.

I shook my head. "No. Dr. Timberlake was shot, was he?"

"He was. Through the head."

I felt obliged to repeat my denial. "I don't have a gun and don't know how to use one."

He said bluntly: "He was shot in the head at point blank range. It wouldn't take much doing. A shotgun was used. A country weapon."

I sat for a moment in shocked silence: he had summoned up such a vivid and terrible picture. "It doesn't sound like an accident," I said.

"It was no accident. I am convinced it was a brutal and premeditated murder."

"There must have been a lot of blood," I said. I don't know why I said it, but the words rose to my lips irresistibly. I couldn't stop myself looking down at my glove. I remember giving my head a slight shake. I swear that until that moment I did not know, consciously, that there was blood on my gloves. God knows what knowledge my unconscious mind had stored up.

I saw him looking, too.

My voice was unsteady. "I tore my hand yesterday. On a thorn."

A look passed between the two policemen. "Could I see the wound, please?"

I held out my hand silently. You could just see the scratch. It seemed a lot of blood for one small scratch.

"May we have the gloves, Miss Brewse?" Silently, I handed them over. "You'll get them back." Harold Lewis was gravely polite. "May I ask you a personal question? Do you know your blood group?"

I told him. It was blood group O, the commonest sort.

After this they did not stay long, having got, I supposed, a little of what they had come for. I didn't dislike them or distrust them, but I felt deeply sad and troubled. I was standing there, still thinking, knowing that I must soon go off to Peterschurch, when I heard footsteps and a dog barking.

I looked up. "Oh, it's you."

"Thanks for the welcome," said Ted Lestrange.

"I didn't hear your car."

He quelled the dog, who went obediently to heel. "I

parked at the bottom of the hill, and walked up." He looked round. "I see I've arrived too late."

I waited for him to go on.

"Lewis has been and gone? I saw his car disappearing over the hill."

"How did you know he was coming?"

"Just guess-work. No, that's not quite true. I've got my contacts. I knew Lewis would be coming this way. He's questioning a lot of people."

"So Lizzie *did* telephone you. I thought she did. I suppose you sent her here?"

"No one sends Lizzie anywhere. You ought to know that." He sat down on a low stone wall.

"You seem to have plenty of people watching me," I said with asperity. "Lizzie, Sylvia Evans, who else?"

He stroked the dog's head. "I'd do it myself if you'd give me the chance. Why not clear out of here, Selina?"

I reacted badly to this. "I don't know why you are hanging around me," I said irritably. "Is it Nun's Castle or me you want?"

"Selina!"

"You can have the Castle. As soon as Lynnet gets back, we will sell it to you and it can be all yours. She's coming you know, coming today. I'm just on my way to meet her."

"What!" He stood up.

"Yes, she is. She telephoned me just now," I said triumphantly.

"Where are you meeting her?" He had a grip on my arm. The dog, too, had risen in an alert way.

"I shan't tell you." The dog moved closer to me. "Call your dog off," I said, my tone deliberately hostile.

He went white and jerked the dog back by the collar. "You can be very offensive when you want to, Selina."

"Then leave me alone. You don't have to protect me. I don't want you to. Leave me alone."

"Don't go. Let me go to meet Lynnet instead."

I shook my head. "I want to be the one to meet and talk with Lynnet before anyone else. And then I'm going to bring her back here."

"Please don't, Selina. You don't know what you may be letting yourself in for." He was pleading with me.

"No, I don't," I said slowly. "But I'm certainly going to find out."

"If I can give you advice," he began.

"No, please don't give me advice." I was still keeping my words deliberately slow. "Because you see, I resent it. I don't like your proprietary attitude toward me, even if it does relate to Nun's Castle and not to me. I can manage the police, and I can manage Lynnet."

"Yes, I see. You've made things beautifully clear, Selina. But unluckily it's not just a matter of personalities."

"Oh, don't be so bloody pompous."

Now I had annoyed him, and I saw his expression change, and for a moment I was frightened. He stood up and the dog moved too. I took a quick backward step.

"Better watch how you drive, Selina, the roads aren't good today." He watched me start the car before he said in a cold clear voice that was a measure of his displeasure with me: "About the dog, Selina, you might have remembered. She's old, she's blind."

I drove away with tears pricking at the back of my eyes. He had found a way to hurt. He always did.

I drove carefully to Peterschurch. I would have done so in any case, but as it was I was quite determined not to get into any trouble that would get back to Ted Lestrange's ears. Thanks to my previous visit, when I had studied the map of the town, I knew the general direction in which I wanted to go.

In a little while I was driving down pleasant side streets lined with trim, small houses, looking for St. Kenelm's Church. This part of the town might be old and poor but it had not been allowed to deteriorate. Then I saw a gray spire rising up ahead of me and knew I had found what I was looking for. I looked up at the church, giving it an assessing glance before I went in.

Within half an hour I was out again, having learned something. In a way, I suppose you could say that I had learned a good deal, but the information I had hoped for was not in my hands.

I think I knew there was something wrong as soon as I set foot inside the church and smelled the strange smell. A smoky, sour smell which seemed to hang in the air.

It had been my intention to put on my professional face and ask to examine the parish records, my pretext being that I was working on the history of a group of local families, a true enough story in its way. Once I was left alone with the records (and my experience had shown me that I would be left to work in isolation) I had intended to check the record of recent marriages.

There was a woman on her knees by the altar when I went in. After a moment's pause she rose and turned round to face me: a tall, gaunt-faced, haggard woman, clad in a long black coat. She looked at me without saying anything. Then, when I had come right up to her, she said: "Are you the press?"

I was surprised. "The press? I'm not a journalist."

"I thought you'd come to take pictures. They said someone would." She saw the astonishment in my face and took pity on me. "You don't know, I see. We've been desecrated." She smiled grimly. "Yes, I can see you're surprised. We've had vandals in. We've had them before."

"What did they do?" I wondered who she was; she couldn't be running the church single-handed. "What happened?"

"This time a fire." Her lips tightened. "*Last* time six or seven louts had a party here. There were cans of beer all up and down the aisle and cigarette ends in the font. The verger found them in the morning all laid out like corpses. They told the police they came in out of the rain."

"It doesn't sound as if they did too much damage that time," I said thoughtfully.

She shrugged. "But it drew attention to us, you see. And now we've had this fire. Oh, it was done on purpose, no doubt of that, the Sisterhood has had problems of that sort before. We attract enemies." She saw my questioning look. "St. Mildburgha's Sisterhood has a House next door, and we use St. Kenelm's for services. At the moment we are having a retreat (just about twelve tired souls). I came across just now to check that nothing *else* had happened."

"What got burned?" I asked, apprehensively.

"All our prayer books and hymnbooks. Some church hangings and some paper flowers that got too dusty to be used. And a great heap of church records. This is a *very* ancient church and some of the documents went back hundreds of years. The Bishop said a lot of what we had should really have been in the Diocesan Record Office, but they've *always* been here," she said. "Still, they certainly would have been safer. I'm afraid it was spite against St. Mildburgha's. We arouse antagonism." She seemed to take a lugubrious pleasure in their arousing hostility, as if it testified to the spiritual force of the Sisterhood, which perhaps it did.

I caught a glimpse of slight, but genuine anxiety in her eyes, and guessed she wondered why I had come. I was surprised she should be anxious. Perhaps she still believed I was a journalist and speculated what sort of publicity I would give her and her friends.

But no, I was wrong, it was a different kind of anxiety. She was studying my face.

"Have I seen you before, dear? Here? No? Just for a moment I thought I *had* seen you."

I moved into the light and she saw me more clearly. "No, of course not, just a passing notion." By now she was curious about me. "Can I help you?"

"I came to check a name in the parish records. It looks as though I'm too late."

"Too late?" She frowned.

"They've all been burned, haven't they?"

"What a sad shame," she said politely. "I'm afraid so."

Yes, I thought, if it *was* indeed a coincidence. It would not have been difficult to create an impression that a gang of boys had broken in and wrought havoc. The local police would be satisfied with a superficial check.

I became aware she was saying something else. She

repeated it. "But we *preserved* everything." Triumphantly she opened a large, carved wooden chest. "We rescued all we could from the firemens' hoses and put them in here. I'm afraid they got wet, though." As the lid was flung open, I saw within a mass of charred and blackened paper. I winced. The worst thing in the world they could have done was to shut that mass of half-burned, half-sodden papers in an enclosed space. By now they would be one solidified mass.

"The County Archivist has promised to give a hand in sorting them," said my new friend in a satisfied way.

"I know him." I nodded. Dr. Mayhew was a good scholar. He would probably have hysterics when he saw what they had done to the records of baptisms, marriages and burials in the parish of St. Kenelm's for the past four hundred years.

I would have a word with the County Archivist, I thought, but not on the telephone. Joan's ears and tongue were too efficient. There were ways of restoring and reading even very charred-looking documents and perhaps it might be as well if Joan never got to hear about them.

But already my mind was moving on from St. Kenelm's, and toward the next thing I had to do, to meet Lynnet, and suddenly nothing else seemed important. To meet my cousin, to be able to talk to her and hear what she had to say became the thing of the greatest urgency. There was a mystery. Lynnet would help clear it up. I knew instinctively it was vital to make contact with Lynnet.

I was wasting time here, the important things were yet to come. I raised my hand to my face as if to brush away a cloud.

"Are you all right?" asked the woman anxiously.

"Oh, yes, quite all right. But I must go."

"For a minute you looked strange."

She must have read something in my face, something I didn't know was there. "I'll say a prayer."

"No, nothing, nothing wrong." I was hardly seeing her, but I said goodbye and thank you. Then I was in the car and driving off. I hope I was polite to her. Belatedly, I realized she was a good woman and that her prayer might have worked.

Within a very few minutes I had reached the town square where the buses arrived. The snow was melting into the gutters and draining away; the pavements looked washed clean. People were hurrying to get home. Buses stopped and deposited passengers, took on a new load and departed again. I stood there with the cold and damp seeping into me. No one seemed to have time or inclination to notice me as I waited for Lynnet. I walked up and down observing.

There was the very special smell in the air that always comes with the thaw after the snow. It was made up of the smell of the trees and the grass on the hills outside the town, and faintly, very faintly, of the sea, because the wind that brings the thaw comes from off the sea.

I was standing there absorbed in my thought, but watchful for Lynnet at the same time, almost enjoying myself. Memories of Lynnet were flooding back into my mind. What a pretty girl she was, especially when she smiled. People said we were alike, but if so, it must have been something in the bone, because whereas Lynnet's colors were all of spring, golden and blue, I was autumn, my hair more russet, my eyes as much green as blue. No one could really mistake us.

I wondered what she looked like now and what she

would be wearing. Lynnet had an eye for clothes and could be relied on to appear looking fashionable and new. I kept twisting my head round for her, but nowhere was that slim eager figure. Somehow I had imagined she would be eager and would run toward me calling my name. But it began to look as if Lynnet was far from eager, almost as if she was reluctant to appear. Could it be that she had already arrived and was sitting waiting for me on one of the benches that lined the square? A cold day for sitting about, but there were a few figures. None looked like Lynnet, though. I walked about, peering in the window of the small coffee shop that stood on the far side of the square. Lynnet might be sitting there, drinking some coffee and quietly observing me from a distance and assessing my mood. It would not be entirely unlike her to do this.

She wasn't there. In the whole square there was no sign of her. I then became aware of what, I suppose, I should have been conscious of before, that the square was emptying of people and that the day was fading into a cold dusk.

I had to accept the fact that either I had missed Lynnet or she had failed to come. I could see a man wearing the uniform of the bus company with an inspector's badge on his collar; I went up to him and asked him if the bus from Hereford had arrived.

He nodded. "Forty minutes ago."

I said, rather lamely: "I was expecting to meet someone."

He moved his cap farther back on his head and tried to be helpful. "The Hereford bus came in pretty sharpish. You may have missed it."

"I was meeting a girl, a young woman."

He looked thoughtful. "Don't remember a girl. But that doesn't mean much. I wasn't looking specially. Lot of school kids. Was she one of them?"

"No, not that young. About my age."

He looked me up and down thoughtfully. "There's another bus comes in from Hereford in about ten minutes. Perhaps she'll be on that one."

I felt more cheerful. "Of course, she could be on the next bus. I'll wait and meet it."

I walked up and down to keep warm. Presently the Hereford bus arrived, and a handful of passengers got out and walked slowly away. The bus prepared to depart.

Lynnet had not arrived. I had to face the fact that she was not coming.

I was alone in the square now, and as the day drew in, it was not a cheerful place. I began to feel frightened, as if I was walking up a dark staircase without knowing what was at the top.

I looked round the square. Although quiet and empty now, it would bloom into life on the arrival of another bus. Surely nothing could threaten me here? But why did I have this strange sensation?

Across the square I saw a figure move out from a doorway. I was watching when the inspector came across. "Not there, eh?"

I shook my head. "No." I was still trying to get a glimpse of the figure moving in the shadows. I didn't think it was a girl.

"There's a stop in the town before the bus gets here. Your friend could have got out there."

"Yes, it could be," I said. I was still watching the quiet,

discreet progress of the figure across the square. It was a man. He had been watching me.

I walked quickly to my car and as I got in I saw the figure enter the telephone box at the corner. His back was toward me, but I saw his hand go out to dial a number. It might be nothing to do with me at all, but I felt the tickle of menace at the back of my neck.

I hated the drive back to Nun's Castle. For the first time I dreaded its emptiness. I was glad the cat would be there waiting. I didn't know what I was going to do about Lynnet. She could communicate with me if she wanted to, and if she did not, then there was nothing I could do about it. Just now she seemed deliberately to have led me to waste my time in Peterschurch. I was worried about her and, at the same time, cross and resentful. As so often with Joe and Lynnet, my feelings were confused. The pair of them possessed to perfection the ability to win devotion and yet alienate it at the same time. I swear I never knew whether I loved Joe or hated him; it was one of the reasons I left Nun's Castle.

I drove fast; there was plenty of traffic on the roads, but as I turned toward Nun's Castle the number of cars grew less and at last I was the only traveler on the road.

The final few minutes of the drive demand concentrated attention as the road curves sharply upward and narrows at the same time. The sight of Nun's Castle bursts upon you suddenly.

I had left in daylight; I had expected to be home before nightfall. The house should be dark and still.

I returned to find a light shining from every staircase window and the top floor gleaming with lights.

The front door was unlocked. Today, contrary to the usual custom at Nun's Castle, I had locked my door. But Lynnet would have a key. Lynnet, I thought, it was Lynnet come after all.

I ran into the hall, calling out "Lynnet, Lynnet?"

Then I halted. I could almost swear I could smell her scent, that light flowery fragrance she had always used. It brought back her face and figure to me even more vividly than the sound of her singing, scents are so provocative. I remember my breathing becoming quicker. I could feel my heart racing.

Then I saw a woman at the curve of the staircase. Her face was half turned away and I could not recognize her, but I knew the pretty red coral coat. Even as I saw her she moved on, up the stairs.

"Lynnet, darling," I called out, springing forward.

I ran eagerly up the stairs, still calling out to her as I ran forward. "Where have you been, Lynnet? I've been waiting and waiting. How did you get here?"

Round the bend of the stairs there was emptiness. She had gone.

I hurried on. "Lynnet, wait for me." By this time I was almost running. "Did you get a train? Or have you got wings? Don't tease me."

All the lights were blazing on the top floor where Lynnet had her room. Across the way the door to her big closet was swinging open. The ancient architects, who had put in the medieval privies, had never realized how convenient these little rooms would be to later generations. Even the topmost floor of all, where the soldiers had slept, and were provided with nothing more than a hole in the floor, had been converted like the rest into a closet for clothes.

I hurried across. "Lynnet?"

I had one foot poised to step into the closet when I stopped short with a cry. Instead of the white painted floor was a gaping blackness, a void.

I tried to grab hold of the door, but I failed. My right foot plunged forward into nothing. I was falling and screaming, plunging to the depths of the tower.

Chapter Seven

My scream saved me, the scream and the old fur coat. All my panic bellied out in that scream and what was left of emotion was just the will to survive. My hands grabbed desperately at the stone walls. The thick old fur coat came up round my waist and, for a moment, wedged me there between the stone lips of the drain. It would not have held for long, but in that minute my hands had reached and grasped a wooden beam supporting the shelves rising above me. Shelves, still bearing innocent piles of sweaters and shoes. Someone, presumably the person who had pushed me, had removed the flooring, so that I was dangling there, with nothing between me and a drop down the stone drain.

I got both hands round the square piece of wood, and braced my back against the stone slope. I tried not to notice that my feet were dangling in space. I knew what I had to do, I had to use my feet to push myself up to where I could climb up onto a shelf. Steadying myself, I moved my right foot around in a probing circle. It was a tiny, ineffectual movement because I was frightened to move. My searching foot found nothing.

I was gripping the wood so hard that it was cutting into the palms of my hands. The pain was a comfort in a way, as a warranty I would cling on and never let go. "I won't let go. I won't let go." I suppose I said the words aloud. I remember hearing them but all the time I was desperately trying to hold back a black shudder at the depths beneath me. The thing I must not think about was the vision of my body falling, falling down the deep well. I knew I was resting at the mouth of a hole through which the force of gravity could suck me with splendid terrible strength.

Once in, never out. I'm sure I did say that aloud. Over and over again in a harsh voice. And all the time, inside me, while all this was going on, was a detached commentator that was taking it all in, even noticing that, under stress, my voice had changed.

I had ripped a fingernail off in my threshing round for a handhold. I could see the blood trickling down my hand. I remembered the fingernail I had found on the floor. There had been violence before in Nun's Castle. I was not the first victim.

I moved my left foot, and this time I tried a bolder, stronger movement, trying as I did so to picture what my foot was doing and where it must move to find the wall. I tried to visualize the relationship of the stonework to my body, and to work out where I could hope to find support. But all I could imagine was the great gap there must be between me and the wall, and the sagging depths beneath.

Also I was beginning to worry if the wood I was holding would continue to bear my unsupported weight: there was no sign of it tearing away, but it could come at any minute. Instead, the crisis came from another direction. My wrists were already throbbing with pain, but even violent discomfort is to be preferred to death. I felt I could take this pain forever, rather than fall into the pit below. But the muscles have a mind of their own. Beyond a certain point I could not control them. I could feel the grasp of my left hand begin to loosen. Although I was still grimly hanging on, numbness was moving into my fingers. There would come a moment when, without anticipation, totally without wishing it, I would suddenly begin to drop.

This was my moment of sharpest fear. But it gave me the push I needed. I pressed my back even more firmly against the stone behind me and using the thick muscles of my rump began to nudge my body upward. My coat came in the way now and clogged my progress up, as it had done downward, but I shoved and heaved, miraculously delivering myself.

As I managed to push myself along I saw that with a little more effort I could draw one knee on to the edge of the stonework by the door and pull myself to safety. It would be dangerous, because I would be stretched between kneehold and handhold, and there must come a moment when I abandoned my grip on the beam and trusted myself to the precipitate forward fall of my body.

I had one knee on the edge and could feel the stone cutting into my flesh. It was a good solid feel and I wanted to go on feeling it. I was fully stretched now and at an awkward angle so that I had no real power to exert to hurl myself out of danger. It was a time for praying, except that I had no breath or energy or thought left. I remember hesitating for a second, hardly daring to move in case my precarious hold was lost, then I recall throwing myself, and reaching, grabbing, grasping, all in one continuous motion.

By a mercy, my hands could get a purchase on the parapet, and hanging, literally by fingertips, I dragged my head and shoulders over the door edge and onto the landing. The rest of me soon followed. And I lay there on the floor, gasping and trembling like a landed fish.

It felt as if hours had passed, but I discovered afterward that the whole episode had taken only minutes.

I was still lying on the floor when I remembered that there had been another person in Nun's Castle besides me, and that this person had meant to kill me.

I got up shakily and examined myself. My stockings were torn, my hands bloody and filthy dirty. My muscles ached. I expect my face looked terrible, but otherwise I was not too bad. Aunt Minny's fur coat, of course, was unscathed.

I knew I had to get out of Nun's Castle that afternoon.

Then I heard movement down below. The unmistakable sounds of a door banging and then the noise of footsteps. Well, at least, I thought, I shall see my attacker face to face this time, and if it's Lynnet then I shall know how to speak to her. I was deeply angry. I felt betrayed. All right, so Lynnet wanted me dead. Perhaps she'd always hated me and Joe too. It could happen. Siblings and kinsfolk did not have to be friends. But I couldn't think what I had ever done to Lynnet to make her hate me so. Except be alive, said a small voice inside me.

Then I thought: I can stand here waiting, or go down and meet her. There was no need to think twice. I have always preferred defiance and I did so now. Indeed, my legs were fairly moving before I knew I had formed the thought.

I smoothed my hair, glad to see that my hands had ceased to tremble. Then I went slowly down the stairs, keeping well against the wall. After that first movement I had heard no sound and on the thick carpet of the stairs it would be hard to hear a footfall.

I crept down, listening. Halfway, I found the little white cat crouching. And she, usually so silent, lifted up her head and called loudly. Immediately a quiet voice called back:

"Selina?"

I walked slowly down the stairs. "Ted."

He stepped forward: "Selina! What *have* you been playing at?"

I went over to a mirror and had a look. I wiped some of the dirt from my face with a handkerchief. This allowed Ted to see my hands. He exclaimed.

"Yes." I looked down at my poor, battered hands. "I suppose it was a kind of game." I suddenly had a vision of my method of levering myself out and how I must have looked. "I dare say I was funny enough. A real laugh." I had the feeling that if I once started to laugh I might not find it easy to stop. So I looked at Ted solemnly. To my horror a tear appeared at the corner of my eye and blinked its way down my cheek. "Damn," I said.

"Selina, my dearest, my darling Selina."

"It's all right. I'm not going to cry." I felt angry now, in good healthy reaction against the fear I had felt. "Someone just tried to kill me." Quickly, I told him what had happened. I didn't choose my words. They just tumbled out. He listened carefully, without comment, but I could read his expression. "I know what you're thinking. You're thinking, that silly girl. I told her to stay out of trouble and she's fallen right in again." I'm afraid my voice wasn't very level.

His voice, annoyingly, was level. "I did tell you to keep the door locked. Presumably you didn't."

"Presume nothing. The person who did this had a key. I'm sure of it."

"Yes, that could be the case," he said. I was glad to be able to detect he was by no means as calm as he looked. I didn't want him to be calm. "Who was it? Did you see?"

I waited for a minute before exploding my bomb. "Yes." I kept my eyes on his face. "It was Lynnet."

"Lynnet!" He swung round on me. "That cannot be. It can never have been Lynnet."

If I had wanted to upset him I had done it with a vengeance. I wondered briefly exactly what he had felt about Lynnet. "I saw her," I said briefly.

He looked at me for a moment, then took my arm. "Come in by the fire and sit down."

Miraculously the fire was still burning. There was no flame, but a good solid heart of fire remained. Ted threw a log on it. "I'll get you a drink." He went over to the table where I kept the bottles Joe and I had assembled between us, and was busy for a minute, during which I could not see his face, but only a forbiddingly stiff back.

I saw the color of the drink he had mixed and protested. "That's too strong."

"Drink it. You need it."

"But you're not drinking yourself."

"Never mind." He sat down opposite me, swinging his

leg. "Now, I think I've got the facts. You came home, ran up the stairs and someone pushed you into a trap. I'll go upstairs and have a look at that in a minute."

"It exists," I said, taking a sip. "In case you think I've imagined it all."

"I don't think that, certainly not. You say you saw Lynnet?"

"I saw her coral-red coat," I said.

He got up to poke the fire, so once again I could not see his face. "Then you certainly did not see Lynnet," he said. "Think, Selina." He turned round to face me. "How did you know it was Lynnet's coat?"

"I recognized it. I saw the coat hanging up." My voice trailed away. "Yes, I see," I said. "Not very clever of me. If the coat was left hanging up, then Lynnet can't have been wearing it when she came back."

"*If* she came back." He stood up. "Are you all right for a minute? Wait here." I heard him running lightly up the stairs. The little cat came down and sat opposite me to wash her face. Soon enough he was back.

"Yes. I've had a look. A nasty, deliberate trap. I'm not sure if it would have killed you, but you would certainly have hurt yourself badly."

The thought of lying helpless and broken at the bottom of that dark pit like a lost doll made me shudder.

"I can't stand dark, enclosed places. Anyone who knows me knows that fact. I tell you it's someone who knows me well. The splinters of glass in my face cream, now this horrible try to kill me. All fixed up by someone who knows how my mind works."

"It could be Lynnet, perhaps." He stared at me moodily. "You didn't tell me about the cream."

I told him briefly. "Just a nasty malicious trick," I said.

"There's a difference in quality between the two episodes, though," he pointed out. "One is wounding, the other murderous. Two people with different motives? Or one person who has become more vicious?"

"One person," I said. "One person who hates me."

"Can you think of a reason why Lynnet should hate? No, that's a silly question, you don't have to think of a reason for hate. It springs out of the hater's own character as a rule."

"Talking of character," I said. "It's out of character for Lynnet to want to kill me just for hate. Unless she's changed a lot, Lynnet is lazy. If she really wants me dead and is prepared to work at it like this, then my hunch is she has a reason for it."

"You have a very good brain, Selina. I like to see it working. Yes, it's a puzzle. I don't see the way clear. We need more information. We'd better get hold of Mallard and tell him everything."

"I don't know if I want him in it," I said sharply. "This is between me and Lynnet."

"Even if you get killed?"

"I don't like Mallard," I said. "Who is he?"

"He's a professional," said Ted, absently.

"I know he's a professional. A professional at what?"

"Just at finding people," said Ted. He went to the window and looked out. "The snow's all gone now."

"That doesn't matter. It'll come back when it's needed."

He was sharp. "Don't talk like that, Selina. You make yourself sound like a witch."

"I am a witch," I said, looking at the cat. "Lynnet and I had a witches' coven, didn't you know?"

He drew his breath in very sharply. "I knew you played some sort of silly games when you were children. Was that it?"

I didn't answer. Let him think what he liked. He could keep secrets and so could I. The cat finished washing her face and started on the delicate area under her tail. She was a white cat and not a black one. Perhaps witches come like cats, black and white, good and bad. She leapt on to my shoulder as if she was indeed my familiar, and from there surveyed Ted Lestrange. It was the first time she had done such a thing. "Clever girl," I said, stroking her. "You *are* learning."

Ted jumped up with an exclamation. "*Don't,* Selina."

"Now I know what you don't like about me," I said. "You like me to be plain, ordinary, clever Selina. But when I show anything that does not fit in with the rules you don't like it."

"Tell me, tell me, Selina, is there any secret you and Lynnet kept together? Is that what lies behind all this?"

"Well, I'm a girl and Lynnet is a girl," I said, deliberately provocative.

"My god, you know I don't mean that. You only had to see Lynnet dancing with the farm boys to know that. But you were always dressing up and acting out histories and pretending to be this and that. Who did you think you were?"

I wanted to answer him seriously, to match his emotion with my own. But pictures of the past moved up in front of me, breaking up and separating and then swimming together again, as if they were images imprinted on water. The past was lapping around me and over me. I could see Lynnet's childish face smiling and nodding to me beneath a wreath of flowers, country flowers, weeds really. Suddenly her face looked wistful and distant. Then there were both of us together lighting a bonfire and leaping and dancing around it in total, uninhibited mirth: there was something burning on the bonfire. Then I caught a glimpse of Lynnet tricked out in some trailing garment and looking somber and serious as she raised her arms and lowered them in a sort of benediction. She looked sublime and mysterious at the same time. How could I have forgotten what an expressive face Lynnet had? She seemed to be trying to tell me something as she danced. Was it a dance? I had forgotten what part, if any, I had played in it. Faces wove in and out of the picture. I was there, and David and Lynnet. Distantly I remember Joe castigating us; he was always a reproving and critical figure. From out of the depths of it all a cry of pure pain rose. I am that child, I thought, out of the fire and darkness I came. I was remembering something more, something about Lynnet. As the game is, so is the child, I thought.

"Ted," I said unsteadily, holding out my hand. What he did then drove all other thoughts from my mind. He drew me into his arms and kissed me. The intensity of my own response surprised me and then delighted me and finally overwhelmed me. The hard sharp-eyed little critic inside me packed up her bags and went away. "I love you." Was it really Ted saying these words to me? But words, for the moment, were not what counted.

When we could talk again, I said shakily: "Witches can't love, you know that, don't you? They can't give and they can't take." I suppose really what I was doing was to set up a defense against what I recognized as an irresistible force.

His voice still muffled in my hair, Ted said, "Don't joke, Selina, not now. It is a joke?"

"Oh, *Ted*," I said. I couldn't keep back the amused reproach. "That wasn't the sort of games we played. But there is something about Lynnet I must tell you."

"Yes, we ought to talk about Lynnet, but not now Selina. Let's have this minute to ourselves. Can we get married soon, very soon?"

"Marriage?" I said. "For a kiss? That's a big price to pay for one kiss."

"Oh, Selina, don't be wicked. You're laughing."

"Well, a little bit." I wished I could be straightforward in my feeling for Ted. I was attracted to and frightened of him at the same time. I didn't want to commit myself. Not with the totality of marriage. I could see I might have to, though; Ted didn't give the impression of a man being easy to stop. "You are solemn sometimes." Pompous I had called it once. Intense, or serious, would be a better word.

"About Lynnet," I began.

"Don't tell me anything," he said; hastily, I thought, if he really did not wish me to amplify anything I had to say about my cousin. "We'll tell all to Mallard."

"Mallard? Why Mallard? What's it to do with Mallard? Who is he?"

Ted said: "I don't know too much about him. He's pretty cagey. No personal details."

I was still pressing. "Why did you go to him about Lynnet?"

Ted left me waiting for a bit, then he said, with some reluctance. "I *was* worrying about Lynnet clearing out. It made things awkward, you know, from the legal point of view. And I *was* thinking of going to an enquiry agent. But in fact, Mallard came to *me*. I misled you about that. I'm sorry, Selina, but he asked me to say it was that way round."

Euphoria was leaving me rapidly. "He seems to have a lot of power, this Mr. Mallard."

"He has." Ted looked wretched.

"He's a policeman, isn't he?"

Ted nodded.

"He must be a very special policeman."

"He is. He belongs to the Special Branch. He investigates treason and subversion."

"And does he think Lynnet was involved in anything of that sort?" I was incredulous.

"No, perhaps not. He didn't let me into his thoughts. But he was looking for her. He wants Lynnet."

"He didn't like me," I said aloud. It was the expression of a thought that had been forming in my mind as he talked.

"You imagine that," said Ted briefly.

"Well, he didn't trust me. What sort of an affair is Lynnet supposed to be involved with?"

"He hasn't said very much. But they know all about her father. He had an imagination full of violence, plots, civil strife, like a Shakespeare tragedy. He *was* mostly imagination, but he did put a bomb where it killed a man. For that he had to run. But don't misunderstand it. I doubt if Mallard thinks Lynnet has done or thinks of doing that sort of thing; but she might be in touch with people who would. Mallard has to keep a sort of register of dangerous people and their contacts. He keeps it up to date. And he doesn't like people on it to disappear. I don't know if Lynnet is such a person. But it could be so."

I hesitated for a minute, and then said: "I don't think Lynnet would ever do anything violent, but she is open to romantic dreams. I remember she wrote a little play once, or anyway, acted it. It was the story of the Harper and the Bride at Llys Euryn. That's not far from here, it's a little bit of local history. The Bride was Gwenllian, the daughter of the Great King Llywelyn, and her husband left her to go to the wars, and never came back. Or apparently was never going to come back. Oh, you know it, it's the story of Penelope and her suitors told in Welsh. The Bride holds off as long as she can."

Was it my fancy or did Ted give me a look?

"But in the end she is obliged to choose a new husband and the wedding is about to take place when a ragged old harper comes into the great hall and plays and sings . . . Of course, he is her husband. She supposed he was dead. That was Lynnet's play. Once I saw her act it to her image in a mirror. Yes, the fantasy could have carried on into adult life. Lynnet didn't have many ideas but those she held tenaciously." It was hard to think of Lynnet being jealous of me, to imagine her as wanting to kill me, but the triangle of me, Joe and Lynnet had been an explosive one. Perhaps there was more buried in it than I knew. Maybe she resented my inheriting Nun's Castle along with her. More and more I was sure the issue revolved around the house and land.

"But one thing I'm sure of, Ted. Perhaps as children we played out this part and acted that part, and perhaps a little of it was carried over into adult life, but we did grow up. I am perfectly adult, Ted, and so is Lynnet. Therefore . . ."

"Yes?" He pressed my hand.

"I am quite sure that whatever Lynnet has been drawn into there is a love affair and a man. Because she is a very simple girl, Lynnet, in the end. Simple and romantic." I was thinking aloud, remembering the letter I had found. "Somewhere in all this is a man that Lynnet loves."

Ted did not answer. I thought at the time he was not listening. I know now he was watching me.

"Can you hear a car?" he said, getting up and going to the door.

"Perhaps it's the person who tried to kill me coming back." I made the remark flippantly, not really believing it. And for the first time I wondered how he himself had arrived so promptly and in such a timely way. "By the way, how did you happen to drop in?"

He shrugged, and I had a quick vision of the man in Peterschurch telephoning, and guessed that I might have been watched. "Did your friend Mallard follow me to see if I did meet Lynnet? You know now that I did not. *Do* you know where Lynnet is? Was she followed here?"

"No," said Ted curtly. "No, she was not followed here, and no, I do not know where she is. I wish I did."

He had his semi-official face on and I thought I knew who was coming to the door. Either the police or his friend Mallard. I knew it by the heavy slam of the car door, the sound of feet on the gravel, followed by the loud steady ring at the door. We had an antique bell ring here and one strong pull reverberated through the house so that we shook.

"It's the police, isn't it? You knew they were coming. It's why you hurried here. Not to protect me or catch Lynnet." I brushed away his protests. "Whatever *is* happening, you are part and parcel of it."

To my spontaneous pleasure, the sight of me, disheveled, blood-stained, and thoroughly kissed, endowed still, I suspect, with a reluctant radiance, stopped Inspector Harold Lewis in his heavy tracks.

"Good Lord, Miss Brewse, what has been happening to you?" He looked at Ted, who, to my secret satisfaction, blushed.

I hid my pleasure in a tart reply: "Someone just tried to kill me."

Lewis's eyebrows (and he had a good thick bushy pair) shot up even higher. I told him briefly what had happened. I didn't know what to make of his reaction; he seemed serious, yet doubtful. I felt he believed me, didn't believe me, understood what had happened, yet didn't know what to make of it, all at the same time.

"Yes," he said. And at once I thought that perhaps I made too much of his reaction. Harold Lewis was not a complex or sensitive man, such shades of meaning as I had sensed were probably beyond him. "A nasty experience for you, Miss Brewse." His eyes went to Ted, then flicked back again to me. I could see he would have preferred Ted not to be there. This struck me as ominous. "May I have a look at the place?"

He went up alone, and returned in a few minutes, dusting his hands on his jacket. "Yes, you could have had a nasty accident there."

I was waiting for him to say: "But all's well that ends well." The words, I am sure, were hovering on his lips but he avoided them. He was blunt enough when he did speak. "Are you sure it wasn't just an accident? You didn't move that wooden flooring (it's no more than a lid) yourself some time earlier and forget you had done so? Or perhaps the servant did?"

I had a momentary brief amusement at the idea of either Lizzie or Sylvia Evans being a servant. They helped, but they certainly did not serve.

"I was pushed," I said firmly. "I saw someone on the stairs. I saw the red coat."

"There's a red coat hanging across a chair in the room below." His voice was skeptical.

I didn't resent what he was implying, but I suddenly felt very very lonely. "Someone came into the house," I said. I was prepared to repeat that indefinitely if necessary.

"But there is no sign of a break-in."

"I suppose this person had a key."

Ted spoke suddenly. "This house is wide open; we all know that."

Lewis spoke to me, and he spoke kindly, as if seeing for the first time the girl his daughter had known. "I can promise you, it will be investigated, Miss Brewse. But it's not my job here and now."

We're coming to it, I thought, and waited.

"You know I am enquiring into Dr. Timberlake's death? I have to ask all sorts of questions. You understand, I'm sure. We are asking questions of all the women who attended Dr. Timberlake's clinic. It's all in confidence, you understand. I've come to you once, now I have come again. You can refuse to answer." He paused, then said: "How well did you know Dr. Timberlake?"

I looked at Ted. "Would you rather be on your own?" he asked.

"No, don't go." I faced Lewis. "I hardly knew him. We met once. Whatever anyone else tells you, that's the truth. But before you start asking me questions, let me tell you something. In America I met with an accident, I'm not quite better yet."

"Please, Selina," broke in Ted, with something approaching anguish.

"No, don't try to stop me. I'd rather talk. I had an accident, perhaps I have periods of amnesia, I don't think so, but I'd be the last to know, wouldn't I?"

"And is that why you consulted Dr. Timberlake?"

"No, it's not, and I suspect you know it's not. You've done your homework, Inspector Lewis. I thought I was pregnant." I didn't look at Ted. It was like stripping myself naked in front of them. But I saw from Lewis's face I wasn't telling him anything he did not know already. The oath of Hippocrates notwithstanding, he had twisted a medical arm at the Peterschurch Clinic and seen Dr. Timberlake's files. He knew more than I did.

"I know now it was not the case. But I don't want you to think it was quite crazy. I had a bit of reason (apart from the fact I felt ill) to believe it a possibility." And, very briefly, I told them both about the marriage certificate sent to me anonymously. I did not tell them about my dreams or about the film of a wedding I had seen.

"What a monstrously cruel thing to do," said Ted. "I knew there was *something* wrong."

"Yes, of course. I suppose I've been going round signaling it to the whole community." I couldn't stop myself sounding bitter.

Harold Lewis continued to look thoughtful. "You should have told us, Miss Brewse."

"Well, perhaps, but would your daughter have? . . . No, I thought not, you hold that sort of thing close to your chest."

He grunted. "Not very wise."

"I investigated for myself. I've made some progress. And I think the fact that I *was* making an investigation got back to the person who sent it and that person arranged a fire at Peterschurch."

"I'd like to see this document if I may," said Harold Lewis.

I got it and laid it before him. "I think this photocopy was made on Lady Dorothy Wigmore's machine."

"You are limiting the area of involvement," said Lewis. "Are you accusing your cousin Lynnet Brewse?"

Ted, all this time, had said nothing, nothing.

"I wish I knew," I said. "But when I telephoned to the Peterschurch Clinic the nurse there thought I was Lynnet. I'm sure of that now. I think Lynnet discovered there that she could never have a child." I did not tell him about the wedding ring I had discovered, but I thought it might have been Lynnet's own. My little fantasies about myself were melting away in the heat of a real relationship with Ted.

Lewis did not comment, thus confirming my suspicion that he had ransacked the Peterschurch records for his own information. "She is a little bit of a mystery, your cousin," he commented. "I used to see her walking round the place and I'd think: I wonder what makes you tick, and I never did find out. I don't know now. You're telling me a little, bit by bit."

"But nothing you didn't really know," I said.

"Miss Brewse, would you like your solicitor here?" Suddenly, he was all official.

"Do I need one?"

Ted stood up. "I ought to tell you that I have asked Miss Brewse to marry me."

Inspector Lewis cast a surprised look at him, but otherwise ignored him.

"Miss Brewse, the gloves I took away have been tested for blood. The tests were positive."

"We both know there was blood," I said. I felt very cold.

"The blood was group A$_3$B. Dr. Timberlake's blood group was A$_3$B. As you may know it is a relatively small group, but with a high concentration in this area. Your blood group is O. It was not your blood."

"Yes, I represent an alien group," I said absently. "I must descend from incomers, and Dr. Timberlake from the indigenous inhabitants."

"Miss Brewse, I'd like you to think how that blood could have got on your gloves."

I shook my head. "Sorry. I don't know."

"Oh, *come.*"

I was silent.

He got up. "I'll give you a day, Miss Brewse. Think about it." He didn't sound aggressive, just rather frightening.

Ted said: "Selina and I are going to be married almost at once."

"Yes, I understand," said Harold Lewis in a quiet tone. "I quite understand, Mr. Lestrange." He walked toward the door. "Talk things over between you. We'll all meet later." It sounded like a threat.

When he had gone, Ted and I confronted each other. "I did not agree to marry you," I reminded him.

He said steadily: "As my wife, you will have a certain amount of protection. I still count for something."

He went away soon after, pausing at the door to give me a thoughtful look, followed by a long kiss.

"Try and remember how the blood got on your glove," he said, as he left.

I nearly went back on the whole thing when he said

this; danger bells were ringing all round me, but the truth is by this time I was sold on the idea.

I wanted to marry him.

Within a day Ted took me round his house to let me see which rooms I would wish to use, and how I would want them redecorated. I already knew his house well, but Ted was, in many ways, a conventional person. His father, and his grandfather (and his great-grandfather, too, I dare say) had taken their brides round the house to inspect and he would do the same. It was expected; it was how he behaved. Nothing could have shown the seriousness of his attitude to me more seriously than this formal introduction to his household. It frightened me. Perhaps I was meant to be frightened. Perhaps that's what it was all about: the Lestranges liked their brides frightened.

We met face to face in the big bedroom furnished by Waring and Gillow in 1880. It was a handsome room with two big windows, one having a view of the village church and the other looking toward a wooded hill. There was a pleasant, straightforward manner to the room, as if the successive ladies who had lived there had got on with their duties as wives and found life agreeable.

Ted sat on the blue chaise-longue and looked round. "Change it if you like," he said comfortably. "Sweep the lot out."

"No, I would not choose to do that."

"It's good stuff."

"Besides, you like it." Old walnut, and blue-brocade hangings, and a pale washed Chinese carpet made a harmonious picture. "You were born here, I suppose?"

"I might have been." He looked surprised. I don't suppose he had ever considered his own birth, or that it had had to happen. Probably he thought of himself as having arrived very much as he was now, Ted Lestrange, in full possession of all faculties and a good seat on a horse. I smiled. He took it for tenderness, for love, and advanced.

"And I suppose you might die here."

"I'm not thinking of that now."

"No." My voice was, of necessity, muffled.

"Am I suffocating you?"

"Very nearly, Ted." I drew away a little, and got my breath back. "Enjoyably, though," I added with a gasp.

"I'm glad to hear you say that," he said, after a perceptible pause.

"Did you wonder?"

"Yes. Anyone would, Selina." He stroked my cheek, softly. "Silly, funny, cold Selina."

"Am I cold?" Strange feelings were stirring within me.

"I don't mind. You'll change."

"Will I?" I asked soberly. "I hope so. I wouldn't want to fail you."

"It's not part of your nature to be cold, silly Selina. You *became* withdrawn and far away. It's part of the bashing Joe and Lynnet gave you."

"You don't like Lynnet, do you? You know I wondered if you were in love with her once."

"I've been after you for ages, Selina, didn't you know? Why did you think I kept coming to London and hanging around?" He had a wonderfully matter-of-fact way of putting things, sometimes. "But as for Lynnet, no, I don't dislike her. She's given me a lot of worry, though, and I call her a silly girl." He frowned.

"We ought to talk about being married," I said, breathless again.

"Ought we?" He frowned. "That sounds more doubtful than joyful, Selina." He could be alarmingly intelligent. Behind his air of being a businesslike farmer and landowner was a perceptive and alert mind. He could be sensitive too.

"I wonder what you expect from me as a wife."

He gave me a direct look. "You know, I think, Selina."

I turned away, not wanting to meet the penetration of that look. He put out a hand and turned me gently back toward him. "Come on, Selina, you're a clever girl, use that bright, efficient brain of yours. What is it I want from you as a wife?"

I said slowly, "Only what I can give, I suppose."

He let his hand fall away. "Right. And that's not so very much at the present, as far as I can see. All right. What you can give is what I want."

"That's quite a compliment," I said.

"Call it that, if you like." Once again, that look, half-sad, half-loving, altogether too discerning.

"It's not just a question of holding or withholding, being generous or being mean-spirited, it's a question of two people being matched—in certain things," I finished, breathless again.

He watched me gravely. "I'll match you."

"It's as well to know." I sat down on the huge bed where several generations of Lestranges had been conceived, born, and died. It was altogether too full of love and birth and then the separation of death. "How many children did your grandmother have?"

"Selina, what *is* the matter with you?"

"I think it's the bed," I said wildly. "There's altogether too much of it."

With a solemn face, he said: "We'll fling it out."

I laughed. Laughter liberates as nothing else can. Spontaneously I raised my face to his to be kissed. "Don't fling it out. I think I rather like this big bed, after all."

There was a deep blue, gilded bedcover and a huge roll of cushions at the head. I fell back upon it, muscles relaxing, happy to be loved, a spring of pure pleasure welling up inside me.

The next period of time could have been a minute, it could have been a millennium. The sun moved round the sky. I saw the golden light reflected in the wall mirror. I thought drowsily: I didn't know the sun was shining till now. Then I remember saying, aloud: "What a *nice* way to behave," and giggling gently. Every sensation was new and fresh. There was no mistaking it: I had not been there before.

I knew then that I could never have been married; that this was a fantasy, a delusion born out of the amnesia and sickness after my accident, combined with the strange pseudo marriage certificate. If I had been in my right mind, I would have rejected it at once.

But inside me some hard core of reason was not conned by pleasure and love. This aloof observer accepted self-knowledge as if she knew it already. It came back to one thing.

I wanted to marry Ted.

Chapter Eight

Then followed a time of great joy and happiness, set, in a lapidary way, between periods of stress and pain. I had to believe this marriage would be real, would truly take hold, and be my life. Only so could I exorcise the weeks gone past. Also, I was in love. I was as surprised at the state as anyone can be who has never been in it before. Flip flop, that was my heart, and I was supposed to be a serious person. What happens to the light in heart then, I thought? They go under in a sea of love, and when they surface again, they find they are a different person, with altered tastes, altered hopes, and even, if a woman, an altered name. But I was plunging in and enjoying my submersion, taking deep gulps of love and feeling marvelous. I was so radiant that it was only afterward I realized I did not really see very much of Ted during this time.

We had agreed that the wedding should take place as

soon as possible, and that Ted should arrange for a special license. Apart from Harold Lewis, our plans were to be a secret. I kept to this part of the bargain. I know now that Ted did not and never meant to.

Meanwhile, I made arrangements to leave Catt's Tower for a few days while I went to London. Sylvia Evans had promised to feed my white cat. I wasn't prepared for David walking straight into the house and surprising me.

"I came to see you before you went away," he said, looking around as if he might see my cases there. "And to stop you if possible."

"I'm only going for a few days." I found myself on the defensive.

"I wish you wouldn't go. You've only just come back."

"How did you know I was going?" I was irritated by the extreme difficulty of keeping anything secret in the valley.

"You ordered a taxi on the telephone."

"Oh, of course." No need for him to say more. By merely picking up the telephone receiver I had alerted the greatest disseminator of gossip in the district, who kept tabs on us all.

He turned toward me, facing me directly for the first time. "I don't want you to go. Please stay, Selina. I love you. I want to love you more. There, I've said it. But I feel as if I hardly know you."

"You've known me for years."

"No. I only knew I loved a girl called Selina who went away. For a little, I confess it, I thought I loved her cousin Lynnet, because she was a reflection of Selina. But you've come back a stranger."

"A stranger you love," I said doubtfully. "I don't want to be loved like that. It's not worth anything."

"It's worth everything," he said. "Give me a chance, Selina."

"There is no chance," I said deliberately.

"I won't accept that."

"You'll learn," I heard myself say.

"You can be hard, Selina," he said. "I'm learning. I've measured that in you already."

We looked at each other. "Go away, David," I said. I remember using that phrase and I can hear my voice saying it. He looked at me and smiled and said, "Well, don't look so sorry for yourself," and I can remember that, too.

There was nothing David could have said just then that could have swayed me. I was mad with love. And to do David justice he didn't try beyond that point. He left me without another word.

I did one sensible thing before I abandoned myself to my dream. I went to the top floor of Catt's Tower and locked the door to Lynnet's room, and then locked the door to the dangerous closet. I did not attempt to tidy up either place, I simply closed the doors on them and left them. Behind the doors might be evidence of my intruder, fingerprints and such like, and one day I might be glad of it.

This done, and Sylvia Evans's queries about the locked doors silenced, I stopped thinking about Lynnet and began to think about myself.

A strange thing happened to me straightaway. I saw it in the mirror. I grew prettier. I thought this odd at first, but I came to the conclusion that it was the first consequence of a happy love affair. Whether it works for everyone or not I am unsure. Ted, at least, seemed unchanged. He said he was happy, though; he said it often, with quiet determination. I was glad to hear it, otherwise I might have wondered. Sometimes he seemed very quiet, and at others I caught him looking at me with a serious, intent look that ought to have troubled me.

He gave me a ring, and when no one was about I wore it. A square sapphire, dark and majestic, fit for a queen. He said it had belonged to his mother. But I was a silly girl and would rather have had some pretty turquoise or little glittery diamond that Ted had bought for me specially and put on my finger. He *did* put the sapphire on my finger, and then withdrew it almost immediately, saying I ought to wear it with a guard ring, as my finger was too thin. I thought of Lynnet's ring hanging upstairs. She would come into my mind, however much I tried to keep her out.

I didn't mean to be a grand, or an imposing bride, but I wanted a wedding dress. I wanted a dress completely contemporary, of my own time. For the moment I had had my fill of the past, and of dressing up, and pretending to be something other than I was. I drove myself to London and went to all my favorite shops in my search for a dress. I visited Liberty's; I looked in at Troubadour, I trotted further afield and visited Robell. But all the dresses that year seemed medieval, with high waists, square necks and long floating sleeves. I seemed haunted by the past. In the end in a small shop, overlooking Hyde Park, I chose a dress of Gina Fraterni's, as pretty as a dream, floating with colored flowers (I didn't want to be a bride in white), fit for the wedding of a fairy queen. I don't think I knew what I had done until I saw myself walk in it, and then I loved my dress too much to change it. Unconsciously I had dressed myself for a dream wedding. I was Titania, after all.

The saleswoman in the shop stood watching me as I stared at my image in the mirror. I had walked from one looking glass to another and now I was reflected in the two. "It's lovely, madam," she said. "You look as if it had grown on you." She smiled at me with a question in her eyes.

I stroked the soft folds. It was just as well she could not read my thoughts, for I was full of contradictions. I was seeing myself in the mirror as I hoped Ted would see me, a loving, welcoming girl, but I was also seeing a stranger. Was this wide-eyed creature really me?

I turned away without answering her. I did not want her to know it was a wedding dress.

"Shall I pack and send?" she asked. "Or will you take it with you?"

"With me." I smiled back, wanting to be friendly. I waited while it was packed, watching the dress disappear under layers of tissue paper.

It seemed to take a long while and as I sat there on a green velvet chair I had time to think. Before I left Nun's Castle I had got in touch with my friend the archivist for the county. I had told him I was interested in reading some of the burned documents from Peterschurch if he could do a restoration job. I didn't tell him any more. Why should I? Anyway, I doubted if he would be interested. From what I knew of him he was a man who lived with and for his work. A worn hole in one of his ancient manuscripts meant more to him than a worm in a freshly picked rose, which he probably would fail to notice. He was a man for whom the past flowered and the present was a desert. He had promised to do his best. His best would be good, and I looked forward to a chance to read the original (and true) marriage certificate. I wasn't sure what I would do with this knowledge when I had it. For, of course, it must be Lynnet's own.

But her husband? Lynnet's own husband, who was he?

Sitting there in my chair, waiting for my wedding dress to be packed, I had a sudden, illuminating thought. Perhaps Lynnet herself had sent me the bogus certificate? What her motives for such an act would be I could not guess. I might understand all this and more when I could read the details on the original certificate. For some time now I had been convinced that the sender was a woman.

I remember feeling glad I had my friend the archivist at work. I had been away from the neighborhood for a long time. I had forgotten how a small community works. I did not know then that the archivist would tell his sister of my request and she would tell Miss Garden, who was the nurse of Dr. Timberlake, and then Miss Garden would, in her turn, tell someone.

My dress ready, I stood up and grasped the box in both hands. I could not help smiling with pleasure as I took it.

"The color goes with your ring," said the saleswoman, with a friendly glance. So then I knew she had guessed.

On the way out I caught sight of myself again in a mirror. I had collected my own fur coat and I could see my face and dark hair outlined against it. I stared silently. Was this really me, this loving, surprised stranger?

I sat in a shop like a small jeweled box and tried new make-up. This was my own private treat to myself. I did not suppose that Ted would notice my face powder had flecks of gold in it and smelt of stephanotis. I dallied happily.

Next to me two women were gossiping as they chose some scent. Both of them were older than I, by about ten years, and from their clothes they were more than ten times richer. I've never minded being poor, though, you enjoy what you've got so much more. With surprise I realized that Ted probably *was* rich. Not superlatively rich (rich rich, as the slang goes), but solidly, comfortably endowed with money, land and chattels. In the distance I seemed to hear Dorothy Wigmore's voice saying: "Old John Lestrange, Ted's father, was what they call a 'warm man,' in other words he left a packet of money, and Ted has shown no sign of cooling the family fortunes; *he* knows how to manage them." I could hear her voice, loud, incisive and somewhat hoarse from shouting too much at her dogs and horses. Underneath, could I detect admiration and a tinge of envy?

I turned over a tray of lipsticks, invitingly displayed. "I'd like something softer, more opalescent," I said absently aloud.

The new color was called Moonglow and it smelt of roses. I loved it, and I bought bottles and pots of rose-scented lotions to go with the lipstick, all packed in deep red and presented to me, finally, in a square silk box. Lovely.

The women were chattering on, using that delicately nasal drawl learnt only in the best schools. Clouds of delicious scent hung around them and they were giggling with pleasure as they tried a new one. I could hear the words through a cloud of Via Lanvin.

"Oh, but of course, we could never divorce. So much of *his* capital is invested in developing *my* land that we daren't even quarrel, let alone separate."

I caught a low murmur from the other woman.

"Oh, yes, it was a love affair," said the first speaker. "He was madly in love with three thousand acres and their mineral rights."

The scent and the words drifted over me and I was receptive to them both. After all, I too was a bride with a dowry.

When I had finished my shopping I sat on a green chair shaped like a slender leaf and drank tea and ate a cake compounded of meringue, marron paste and whipped cream. One thing I did not have to watch was my figure. In fact, I could probably do with a bit more weight. Earlier that day I had seen my London doctor and been given a good report. I felt cheerful and fit. My little flirtations with amnesia seemed over. There were certainly problems to be faced, but I reckoned I could face them. My mind, anyway, was working well and that's always a good feeling.

I knew I had spent a lot of money in the last few hours and I did not feel guilty, although I very often did when I was extravagant. As well as my dress, I had a silk negligee that had a Paris label and some slippers that matched. I had a simple suit to wear when I departed on my honeymoon. I supposed I would *have* a honeymoon. I must check with Ted on that. But if and when I left for this hypothetical honeymoon I had a new set of Gucci luggage in which to pack my possessions.

I thought for a while about my possessions. I did not seem too well endowed with worldly goods, but there was nothing I owned that would be a disappointment to Ted or a surprise; he had long known as much, if not more, about my finances as I did myself. Beside's Nun's Castle and a small number of investments, I owned a few valuable books and the chance of a career. We had discussed my own work, Ted and I, and agreed it should go on. He wanted me to have my own life, he said, and I was never to put him first. He sounded very unselfish and a little remote. I wondered if I meant as much to him as he had begun to mean to me? He wasn't easy to fathom.

In a few short days I was back at Nun's Castle. Ted and I telephoned each other constantly, but our meetings were brief. He said, half-jokingly, half-seriously, that it was always a busy time when a man was about to get married.

There were no more calls from the police for the time being. In spite of their earlier threat of action within twenty-four hours. I supposed that my engagement to Ted had made a difference, although I knew well from the gossip of Sylvia Evans that they were still actively investigating Dr. Timberlake's death. They still had my gloves.

I heard no more from Lynnet, and I took my own wary precautions against any more possible attacks. I kept to the house, and occupied myself with clearing up small matters in my own work. The little cat seemed glad to have me back. It had grown much bigger while I was away.

Three days of peace, one, two, three and then on the fourth day . . .

I heard the bell ringing in the Chapel, ringing this time with a quicker, more cheerful note. Harry the bellman must be in a happier mood.

On an impulse I put my coat on and walked over. I took my time, enjoying the walk. The warm weather had gone, not to return this year, but the snows had melted and the sky was a deep, cold blue. It was a lovely day if you were warmly dressed and well fed. For the first time I wondered if Old Harry was well looked after and who was responsible for him.

I scrambled up the last slope and turned toward the Chapel. The bell fell silent. He'd seen me, I suppose. I already knew he watched from a side window of the bell tower.

He was waiting for me inside the door. I think he was glad to see me, because he smiled. "I was ringing the bell for you."

"For me?"

"For you: you are to be wed."

This was my first intimation of how widespread was the news of my wedding, and how very far from being a secret. He had an archaic way of putting it, but he had the position clear.

"Yes, I am," I replied. "Who told you?"

He looked vague, and I thought for a moment he was going to say he'd heard it from the bees, or the birds had told him. Instead he said: "Lady Dorothy. Lady D., it was."

So Dorothy was back, and up to date with information as usual. Still, it surprised me she should gossip with someone so far below her in the social scale. Dorothy observed certain rules in behavior, and distance was one of them.

"She told Phoebe and Phoebe told her sister and her sister told me," said Harry as if reading my thoughts. "I was doctoring Phoebe's little cocker bitch that the vet couldn't do nothing with. I brought her round, though. *Worms,*" he said with emphasis. "Any fool could see it was nought but worms." He gave me a sweet smile and returned to the bell tower and presently I heard the bell playing a merry little jig. All in my honor, no doubt.

There was a strong wind blowing (it had been blowing ever since I returned to Nun's Castle), and the chapel seemed alive with strange noises. The windows creaked and little puffs of air came from the center aisle, bringing with them a smell of past centuries of dust, as if the air had never moved till now.

A particularly shrill draught was running under the wall painting by which I lingered for a moment, wondering if I would ever master its secret.

Along the same wall as the painting was placed a dark oak chest with a carved lid. Idly, I opened it.

At first I saw only clothing, and then as my observations continued I realized the box was full of pale-colored, sumptuous, *new* clothes. Slowly, I pulled out first one garment, then another, and I thought to myself: these are the clothes worn by the man and the woman in the film of a wedding.

I looked up. Old Harry was far away in a world all his own. He would not notice what I did. Or so I thought.

I plucked out the bride's dress and retreated to the antechapel, where linen-fold screens of dark oak gave privacy. I pulled off my own plain woollen and drew the stiff damask over my head. It seemed to fit me perfectly. I found myself thinking uneasily that it might almost have been made for me. And yet it did not suit me. I knew, without even having a mirror in which to look, that I seemed stiff and uncomely in this archaic dress, which was both made for me and yet not made for me.

The edges of my happiness had begun to crumble.

I was replacing the garment in the wooden box when I became conscious of the old man staring at me.

"What clothes are these?" I asked him.

"Some things of Lady Dorothy's, I daresay. I never saw them before. But everything here is hers," he said. "The chapel is hers. And the land it stands on. And I'm hers when she wants. She's been very good to me, has my lady. And she says *that* gown is the Princess's wedding gown."

"So you *do* know what they are," I observed.

"Only what I'm told." I could see I had embarrassed him and he did not, for some reason, wish to tell me about the clothes. And yet he could not stop talking. "Well, it's all been a mistake you see, the wedding that was not a wedding. I told them at the time it was all wrong, but they wouldn't have it." He looked at me for a minute, and then said, with a kind of sweet gravity, "For 'tis playacting when all is said and done."

He was a completely sincere and honest old countryman and would speak the truth. I knew that I was on the verge of a discovery.

Then, to my fury, the great door of the chapel was pushed open and Lady Dorothy arrived in a flurry of wind-blown leaves.

She seemed irritable. "Hello, there, Harry, what are you doing here? Be off home now, before you get a cold and have us all looking after you. Remember last winter." She gave me a brief nod. "Hello, Selina."

Harry bundled his coat round him and obediently made to go. "I be off to Davies's," he said.

I broke in. "Wait a minute, where do you live? I'll drive you home." I resented for him the brusque way Lady Dorothy had sent him off like an old dog.

"Oh, he lives up in the hills at Davies's," she answered for him impatiently. "He can easily walk. You can, can't you, Harry? It's easier to walk by the footpath than drive by the road."

I demurred. "All the same," I began, but the man himself interrupted me. "I prefer to walk up to Davies's," he said. "It stretches my legs." They looked as though they were stretched enough, I thought, his face seemed tired. "And I dunno what they'd say to me arriving in a car. They're not fond of visitors at Davies's."

"Off you go before the rain comes down," commanded Lady Dorothy.

I watched him shuffle off. It was plain that neither of them wanted me to be alone with him, but I am not easy to deflect, and I made up my mind I *would* talk to him and question him. So I turned a mild face to Lady Dorothy. She seemed in a bad mood.

"Nice to see you, Selina," she said, not looking as if it was nice at all. "So you're getting married." It was not a question but a complete statement.

"You know then?"

"Everyone knows," she said shortly.

"I suppose that's Ted. I thought we were going to keep it secret."

"When I said everyone, I meant everyone in a *small* circle," she said.

"Everyone who *counts,* do you mean?"

"You make that sound nasty. No, my dear, I just meant all your friends."

I nodded. Farewell friends, and welcome foes, then, I thought.

"You mustn't take what I say amiss, my dear. I'm glad you're marrying Ted. Your interests *match,* after all."

"What does that mean?" I could feel a flush of anger beginning to rise in me.

"You must know that with Nun's Castle and his estate joined together you two would have complete control over the copper deposits. There's quite a lot of copper there, my dear, and copper is getting scarcer. It will be quite worthwhile having it mined."

"The copper has always been there," I said defensively. "But it's not been worthwhile getting it out."

"Modern mining techniques *and* the insatiable modern demand for it have made it worthwhile," she answered impatiently. "You're in the past, my dear. Ted isn't. I hand it to him."

"Ted is not marrying me because of what I own," I spoke slowly, but already, inside, I was wretched.

"No, no, of course not. I wouldn't suggest it for a minute. Still, it's nice that it works out as it does."

"He would have *said* something about the copper," I said.

"*Hasn't* he?"

"No."

She was blunt. "I'm surprised, then. It's what's been taking him to London so much.

"Where are you going?" she said hastily, as I started to move.

Dorothy could be very stupid sometimes. There was only one place I could be going.

I had been to the Lestrange house once or twice since our engagement, and in any case, I knew Ted's habits. He worked in his office there in the mornings, dealing with estate matters. He would almost certainly be there now.

His office was empty when I got there, but his big black Labrador dog lay by the fire and greeted me with a soft warning growl.

"It's all right, Pan boy," I said soothingly. He was called Pan because his mother, now blind, had been imported from North America at some expense; she had flown by Pan-Am. This was the sort of simple joke Ted went in for. Pan's manners were excellent, but he did not like me, or was jealous of his master's interest in me, and was not above showing his feelings when Ted was absent.

The room was filled with sunlight and I could smell the scent from a big bowl of hyacinths. The flowers were the only feminine touch in the room, though, which was otherwise strictly masculine and untidy. The wallpaper and curtains looked as though they had been put up in his grandfather's time, and consequently were now coming back into "chic." The desk and heavy chairs were certainly old enough to count as antique, but looked as though they had been kicked and scuffed by several generations of large men, which was what the Lestranges were.

I heard the dog growl again and I looked round. "Hello, David. Are you looking for Ted?"

David Griffith smiled. "Hello, Selina. It's nice to see

you. You look prettier than ever. No, I'm not looking for Ted. The other way round. He telephoned and asked me to call."

"I wonder why he did that?"

"I don't know." He paused, as if making a decision. "I think I ought to tell you, Selina, that Ted and I have long since ceased to be friendly. If we ever really were. Our paths have drawn right apart. And that happened long before you came into it."

I said gently: "*Do* I have to come into it, David?"

"Yes, I think you do. You come right into it, as you know very well. How could I keep you out?" He held my shoulders and turned me gently to face him. He looked at me lovingly for a moment, then abruptly released me. "Anyway, if the information means anything to you, you certainly haven't improved our relationship."

Hesitantly, I said: "I don't know if it does mean anything to me. Or if it ought to do. I'm going to marry Ted."

"And you really want to marry him?"

I drew away. "I am a free agent, you know. Ted doesn't use hypnotism."

He sounded angry. "I wonder if he doesn't."

They had been friends once, perhaps not deep or close friends, but men who liked each other. Now, from David, at least, came only anger. Ted was, as always, more difficult to read. It could not be all my fault.

As I stood there a strange feeling swept over me as if, in spite of what they said, neither man truly loved me for myself, but was interested in me for some other reason. I shook my head to drive the thought away.

"You're a strange girl, Selina," said David. "If anyone

has hypnotic powers, it's you. Don't you see you fascinate us all?"

I had teased Ted with the fancy of me being a witch, but now the joke was over, and I was not amused.

"I think it's Nun's Castle that fascinates you all," I said. "Not me." Oh, Lynnet, Lynnet, I thought, where are you? You are part-owner of the Castle, after all. "Are you interested in copper deposits too, David?"

I saw he knew what I meant, for a bleak look came over his face. "It would be a crime to despoil the land here. It's a sacred trust and ought to be kept."

"That's coming out and saying it." In spite of myself, I was amused. David hadn't changed so much then, still the same romantic, half in love with the past.

"You agree, don't you, Selina? Where do you stand?"

I wasn't going to be pinned down in this way. "I don't know, David, don't push. It would mean jobs for men who need them."

"The land is our heritage. Future generations will blame us if we ruin it for them."

Yes, I could see that David would be on the side of the environment rather than material wealth, whereas Ted might take a different position. For myself, I couldn't help remembering the real poverty of the valley and the needs of the men who labored there.

"Don't stay, Selina, go away. Don't stay here and marry Ted. You will, if you stay here. Clear out fast."

A cold trembling started inside me, and was repressed. "Like Lynnet?" I asked. "Run away from Ted? Was that what Lynnet did?"

"I never said anything about Lynnet."

"I can see a connection, though."

It was too late to run away from Ted Lestrange even if I wanted to, because he was in the room. He stood there with all the assurance of a man whose forebears had entered the room as owners for the last seven generations.

I was sorry for the moment that David was present. When you are planning a scene with a man, an audience is not desirable.

"Hello, Selina, I wasn't expecting to see you. 'Morning, David."

His eyes were welcoming, but his voice was careful and guarded. Too many strings attached to too many puppets seemed to lead to Ted Lestrange. Was he really a puppet-master?

I looked into his eyes, trying to assess the welcome he had put there. "Hello, Selina," he said again. "I'm glad you came. I've got you a wedding present." He put a paper-wrapped box on the table.

So he too wanted a scene, but of a rather different kind, and was solving the question of an audience by ignoring David. He leaned forward to kiss me; I turned aside. He hadn't learned, perhaps would never learn, that I did not like to be made love to in public. David caught my eyes, and must have read appeal there because he took a step forward.

I spoke abruptly. "I thought our wedding plans were to be a secret."

He made a demurring noise. "Well."

"Everyone knows."

"No, I may have let one or two people know," he said with a grin.

"Let's have a moratorium on marriage," I said.

"What's that?"

"What do they call it when the banks close and they declare a holiday on repayments?"

"A moratorium," he said slowly, his look beginning to be by no means friendly.

"So that's what I said. I want to close the bank temporarily. I mean I want to postpone our wedding."

His face was stony, and I began to feel a little frightened. "Why?" he said.

"I want time to think over the relationship between our marriage and the mineral-property rights vested in the Nun's Castle estate," I said. I suppose if I'd worked on it for years I couldn't have hit on a way of phrasing it that was more insulting, but of course I wasn't trying to be insulting, I was just speaking out of the pain and hurt that encompassed me. "I want to be sure what I'm being married for."

"Don't go too far, Selina."

I didn't need the warning. "I'm going back to Nun's Castle and I don't want to be disturbed. I'm going to shut myself up there and think."

"Selina, don't be so blind. Can't you *see* what's really going on? Selina, wait. Please wait."

But I was past listening or waiting. Inside me a voice was whispering that I was indeed going too far, but I was driven by something outside myself. I brushed past him, knocking the table as I did so, and the present he had brought me went banging to the floor.

I suppose some piece of mechanism must have jerked into life because a gay little tinkle of music, like a silver rose, immediately flowered at my feet. I sprang back. "What is it?"

Ted leaned forward to pick it up. "A musical box. I bought it for you."

The music was still tinkling out, a beautiful, sweet, old-fashioned sound. But the tune was "Cherry-Rype," Lynnet's song. Then it stopped.

Memorials of Lynnet seemed to spring out of the ground for me as I walked. This one was too much for me now.

I turned to face the two men. From causes I could not begin to explain to myself, I felt equally angry with them both. "Goodbye. Don't try to follow me. For reasons that are private and personal I am off marriage for the moment. I'm going back to Nun's Castle."

My time of happiness was over: the time of iron had begun again.

Chapter Nine

The bad things started to come at me as soon as I got back to Nun's Castle. An evil wind tugged at my skirts as I ran from the car. Little arrows of sleety snow came with the wind. If the snow fell this time it would be black snow, steel gray as it lay, tinged with the dirt from the furnaces and stacks of the industrial towns to the north-east. I could tell by the direction of the wind. I hated the days of black snow.

Inside the hall, the great door slammed against the buffeting wind, I saw a note in Sylvia Evans's writing propped up against a bowl of flowers. Now that I knew that Sylvia was, in a sense, a spy planted on me by Ted, I had invented a game which I played and she didn't, about never telling her where I was going or why. It didn't matter: she knew, anyway.

"I tried to get you at Mr. Lestrange's, but you'd just

left. The policeman says will you telephone him about your gloves. Number written down. The cat's fed, and I'm off to give my husband his dinner. He can't fancy his food unless I'm there."

I imagined I detected a touch of smugness there; I put the note down, and dialed the police number. Soon I was speaking to Superintendent Lewis; he sounded dovelike and sweet.

"Miss Brewse, you never signed a statement admitting that the gloves I took possession of were yours, did you? Will you just come down here, please, and identify them as yours and sign such a statement?"

I had thrown off Ted's protection now, and was on my own. My heart sank. "Yes, I'll come," I said. "Will this afternoon do?"

"Any time, any time, my dear," he said jovially. "But Miss Brewse . . ." I waited to hear. "Don't leave it too long."

I knew what it all meant. I might have led a quiet, sheltered life, but I saw the slow official movements toward forming a case against me. My own statement, if I made it, would form an important part of the police case.

I made an immediate resolve *not* to hurry down to see Superintendent Lewis. It was my first, important, life-saving act.

On an impulse, I used the telephone next to call Lady Dorothy Wigmore. Phoebe, her secretary, answered and then I heard her having a low-voiced conversation off-stage. For a moment I thought she was going to pretend Dorothy was not there, but no, immediately I heard her employer's voice, full of accusation.

"Selina? What did you run away for?"

"Not away, Dorothy, but *to*. I ran to find Ted."

"Oh, *well*." She was at once indulgent. Young love, I could almost hear her thinking. I did not explain to her that it was not love but anger that had made me run. Instead, I embarked at once on my questioning. I managed to put a little edge of confidence and certainty into my voice; this was always wise with Dorothy.

"You had another medieval charade up at the chapel, didn't you? One that you didn't tell me about? It was a wedding."

"Yes, Selina." She sounded reluctant. "It was before you came back. Joe was going to film it for me. It was the start, really. Then we had a quarrel, and he wouldn't do it. Phoebe took a film, though, and gave it to him."

"I know. I've seen it."

"It was a good idea. I had the clothes copied from a Memling picture in Bruges. The ceremony I got out of *The Golden Rules of Medieval Manners*."

"I know the book."

"But everyone quarreled. Lynnet had already run away. It was a bad time. I tried to bury it." She sounded uneasy, furtive, as if she had been engaged in dubious sexual behavior and I had somehow found out. I saw, for the first time, what a deep emotional hold all her romantic charades had on Dorothy. She was deeply involved.

"Who played all the parts, Dorothy?"

"No one you know, my dear Selina. I got professionals up."

She was lying: I did not believe her for a moment. If I made up my mind it was important to me, I could dig away at Dorothy and make her talk, but it would take time. I could hear Phoebe muttering in the background and I heard

Dorothy give a protesting "No" in a loud, explosive tone.

I guessed then that Phoebe had heard her lying and tried to get her to tell the truth. "Why don't I ask Phoebe?" I thought.

I sat there thinking for a moment about Phoebe. She was such a quiet, hard-working girl that she got overlooked, but she was there all right in the background of my life and Lady Dorothy's, making her protest for the truth. She was uncorrupted.

I found that word had a strange flavor on my tongue, but it seemed the right one. I tasted the flavor again and found it disquieting.

Phoebe was a little, still, quiet voice of rectitude. And she had loved Joe. The minute the thought flashed into my mind I knew it was true. Why shouldn't she love Joe? She had known Joe for years and he had been an attractive man. I was coming to see that, for almost everyone except me, he was lovable.

Thinking of Phoebe reminded me of old Harry, who had cared for Phoebe's dog. I wanted to talk to him. He, like Phoebe, was a point of truth.

I sat for a moment, thinking, then I got up. Moving the little cat, who had sat herself carefully in my lap, I went to the big window. High on the hill beyond, I could see a small house. I imagined this was Davies's Farm, where Harry stayed. I could make out a tiny footpath winding up the side of the hill. I could imagine myself walking up it, my heart pounding, the cruel wind blowing in my face. I imagined myself returning, illuminated.

Reality is never what you expect. The essential

unpredictability of the human situation is both its most hopeful and its most daunting quality. Nothing was as I imagined it with my visit to the Davies's Farm, and yet illumination, of a sort, I received.

The Davies's Farm was more of a small holding than a farm to be spoken of in the same breath as the Lestrange farm, which was, I suppose, an estate. A *place,* as the Edwardians called it.

I had followed the path easily from where it dove down the hill to end near the river. I was surprised how quick and easy I found the ascent. The path must be in regular use, although except for a few black-faced hill sheep I met no one. I had plenty to think about as I walked, such as how I would introduce myself to the Davieses, what I would say to Harry, and how I would phrase my questions without alarming him. I knew he must not be alarmed.

I could see the old reservoir from where I stood. It was an ancient affair, what was known as an impounding reservoir, gathering together a supply of the river water and holding it behind puddled walls before letting the river pass on over a weir. Now that I knew where to look I could see where one wall had been patched after the bomb incident. I wondered how much it had been weakened by the blast and what happened if the river were in flood.

I stood on the crest of the hill and looked down to where, beyond a belt of trees, I could see the roofs of the chapel and Nun's Castle. Even farther down I could see the curve of the river showing like a dull silver thread in the winter landscape. I was looking down on Ted Lestrange, David Griffith, Lady Dorothy and Superintendent Lewis. Down there Dorothy was dictating letters to Phoebe, Sylvia Evans was feeding her husband and Ted was doing what?

Slowly I moved toward the farmhouse. It was fairly run down and dejected, as if prosperity was not just round the corner and had not been for years. I knew these small farms, it took back-breaking hard work to keep them trim.

The house was old, very old, and looked as though it had stood there through the centuries and rested its walls on foundations even older. This was true: a farmstead had been here when iron was a new metal. Even the ghosts were haunted on soil like this.

As I came up to the house I heard music, a lovely, romantic sound, a Viennese waltz. I pushed open the door and went in.

A woman was sitting in a small armchair, hands loose in her lap, eyes far away in a dream. The music rolled round the room, completely enclosing her. Then she heard me and stood up.

I can't say she moved hurriedly, rather slowly and with some dignity. She was my height and my size; I guessed we were about the same age, but we had lived in different worlds. We stared at each other, two lonely girls, wondering what to make of each other.

"I'm Selina Brewse," I said. "I've come to talk to Harry. He does live here?"

She nodded in assent. "I'm Nesta Davies. You won't find him, though."

I was disappointed, irrationally, powerfully disappointed.

"He's had a heart attack and gone into hospital. You must have passed the ambulance on the road."

"I walked," I said.

She nodded. "Like Harry. He came hurrying up the

hill. I told him not to. You'll kill yourself, Harry, coming up like that, I told him. No notice."

I swallowed. "Will he die?"

"No, I don't think so." I suppose I looked doubtful, because she said, "You can trust what I say. I've had some nursing training."

"I feel responsible for causing him to hurry up the hill. I had a conversation with him that may have upset him."

"He'd have done it, anyway, I expect." But her tone carried no comfort. She wasn't exactly hostile, but she did not like me.

The shock of hearing about the old man's illness had blurred my reactions to Nesta.

"I know you, don't I? That is . . . I've seen your face, your portrait. It is you who stands as the Princess in the wall painting in the chapel."

"Yes. Lady Dorothy thought I'd look like she did. And I expect I do. I'm local stock."

"Like me," I said absently.

"More than you." Her voice was strong. "Centuries upon centuries my folk have lived here. I believe I'm descended from her, herself. She was the Prince's daughter and a king's granddaughter, and when her father was killed in battle she was put in a monastery. But she escaped and married into a local family and many of us round here are descended from her." Her voice was high.

"It could be." My voice was professionally aloof. No one knew better than I did how hard it was to establish an accurate genealogy, and what dreams of royal descent people allowed themselves. If something did not happen to bring the whole false edifice tumbling down, then you could go on deceiving yourself for years.

Nesta gave me a look of flaring dislike, which I accepted humbly: it seemed the only thing I could do. I did not want to assert myself against this simple country girl any more than I had to. "You were also the bride in one of Lady Dorothy's first attempts to recreate a medieval scene."

No wonder the dress had fitted me: Nesta and I were the same size. And no wonder the dress had not been becoming to me: I am dark-eyed, and the dress had been designed for a girl with bright blue eyes and flaming hair.

The music, which had been turned low, burst out again in a flow of melody, carrying us both with it and surrounding us with emotion and beauty. I was daunted and silenced. I have always been very vulnerable to music.

On a chair across from where I stood there was a crumpled blue baby shawl. It was a shock, and yet not a shock, if you know what I mean. The sight of it there seemed all quite inevitable as if what would be, would be, and what must be would certainly take place.

"You going, then?" said Nesta.

"Yes." I turned blindly for the door. "I'll go back the way I came. But tell me first: did you leave a baby at Nun's Castle? And did you then take him away? I think you did. Why?"

Nesta said coolly: "Take care how you walk on the path. It's slippery and more dangerous than you might think. About the child—I'm not a silly, neurotic girl. I act on reason. The child was where he had right to be."

"Is he your own child? Or my cousin Lynnet's child? Could he be?"

She didn't answer, but a look in her eyes reminded me of the child. They had too much in common those two, not to be blood kin. Lynnet's blue eyes were more gentle.

"Watch the path," said Nesta. "You don't look strong enough to stand much."

"I'm very strong," I said angrily.

"That's not what I've heard," said Nesta, turning away.

"I'm strong enough for you," I said. I don't know why I said what I did, but I suddenly knew it was true. I had inside me a little bag of fortitude that would see me through.

I went through the farmyard toward the downward path. Somewhere in the house behind me, if I opened doors and looked in rooms, I would have found my friend, the silent, blue-eyed baby. Like mother, like child, I thought, enigmas both.

As I turned to give a last look, I saw a man crossing the yard. He wasn't looking toward me and perhaps had not even noticed me. He was a tall, thin figure with hollowed cheeks and flapping gray hair. His shoulders were bent and his thin wrists projected from the sleeves of his coat. Enigma number three, I thought.

I changed my mind about walking back down the footpath and turned toward the road. The wind was picking up cold damp handfuls of air and throwing them at me. Head down, I trudged on. Rain was falling heavily. I discovered within myself a mood of fighting defiance. For a few hours I would forget Ted, Dorothy, the police and their investigation, and go back to Nun's Castle and wrestle with the problem myself. I was sick of being given orders in one form or another. I heard a car behind me and moved closer into the hedge. The car passed me, then slowed, and a woman's voice called out: "Want a lift down the hill?"

"Yes, please." And then I stopped. I think she was as

surprised to see me as I was to see her. "We met at Dr. Timberlake's, didn't we? You're one of his nurses." And the one who doesn't like me and who thinks I may have killed him.

"It's Miss Brewse, isn't it?" She sounded unsure of herself, as if the dislike she had felt for me had drained away, leaving doubt in its place. "I didn't expect to see you."

"I've been to the Davies's farm. I wanted to see old Harry, but he's ill. Nesta Davies says he will recover."

"Oh, she'd know. Nesta would have made a remarkable nurse if she'd finished the training."

"But she didn't?"

"No. She could never bear to be away from home. Her father was the same."

"There are people like that," I said, thinking of Emily Brontë and her sister Charlotte, people who sicken and die away from their native soil. So Nesta was not just the simple country girl I had thought her.

"Get in. I'll be glad to drive you down." It wasn't difficult to see that she was trying to offer me a sort of apology. "I was not too nice to you on the telephone, my dear. Shall I say I'm sorry? I was beside myself with distress at the time."

I was touched by her sincerity. "I can understand that, you must have been fond of Dr. Timberlake."

"Yes. I was. He was a good man. He had his own rules, but no woman who came to him for help and treatment got anything but the best he had to give."

I watched the hedgerows skim by; she was driving fast and well.

"The doctor was shot in the back of the head with a shotgun while he was sitting at the wheel of his car. A shotgun is the weapon someone brought up in the country would know how to use. Any woman from round here would know how."

"I suppose that's true."

"Oh, it is. The police know Dr. Timberlake had expected to meet a woman. He told me so. I thought it might be you. I apologize."

"I called on Dr. Timberlake as a patient," I said deliberately. "I had good reason to see him. Or so I thought. I don't see why that qualifies me to be the murderer."

"I didn't think you shot him. I thought it might have something to do with you. I was so upset when you called on him as a patient. He'd had so much trouble with your cousin."

I kept my voice quiet. "Yes. I knew Lynnet had been to see him. The first time I telephoned, you thought it was she again, didn't you? Won't you tell me all about it?"

Her voice rose hysterically at once: "I don't know anything. There's nothing to know."

"I think there's something. Something that concerns my cousin Lynnet and her disappearance."

"I don't want to talk about it."

We were already at the bottom of the hill. I would have to get out here and walk up a short lane to the front of Nun's Castle, which I could already see.

"What *was* Dr. Timberlake involved with? There was something." I remembered Lady Dorothy's voice: "The Abortion Center for the County."

"Nothing. He was a good man. He thought of nothing but medicine."

"*Then what are you mixed up in?*" I said softly.

I knew I had struck home from the ugly flush that

arose in patches on her neck and cheeks. She was a nervous, worried woman, easy to alarm. I didn't get out of the car, but just sat there, waiting for an answer.

"As if you didn't know," she said.

"I *don't* know."

"I'll call tonight and talk to you." Her voice was unsteady. "Tonight, remember. Don't go out."

"Thank you. I'll be there." I got out of the car. The gears were ground together, the car jumped and then shot away.

I plodded home. Suddenly, I was ravenously hungry.

Nun's Castle with all its ghosts and secrets gave me its usual ambiguous welcome. I opened the door and felt the past rush out to meet me with the warm air from the house. The more hints I was getting about the lives of my two cousins, Joe and Lynnet, the sadder I felt. I could never make up the loss of my love and affection to Joe. Perhaps I could do so to Lynnet? Meanwhile I would pay back some of my debt to Nun's Castle by continuing my work on its archeology. I had never entirely abandoned it, giving some attention to it, even at my most preoccupied moments. I had mapped out the ground plan of the old castle, filling in all sorts of details, left vague in the hitherto published maps.

I had wondered, expected almost, that Ted would try to find me and talk to me, but he left me alone. I was half-pleased, half-annoyed. Perhaps I thought that I *ought* to have been sought out. I was glad, however, to receive no call from Superintendent Lewis. All around me I had the feeling of events working themselves out to a conclusion, and I sensed that in the whole scheme of what was happening police activity was irrelevant.

The wind kept up and I could hear it howling round the house. Every so often it gave a roar, then fell silent for a minute. The wind lives in these hills and in winter gains strength and voice and identity. This was the north wind, the wind of the cold dragon. And the rain still fell.

The telephone rang once and when, reluctantly, I answered it, I heard David's voice. He sounded concerned and anxious. "Don't stay up there on your own. I don't like it. Why not come here?"

"No, thank you. It's kind of you, but no, thank you." I hated David's gloomy bachelor establishment at the best of times, now the thought was fearsome.

He was tactful enough not to offer to visit me.

It took me a little while to settle into Nun's Castle again. I had the uneasy feeling of people having come and gone in it while I had been shopping in London. The feeling grew so strong that eventually I picked up the telephone and rang Sylvia Evans.

She seemed embarrassed when I asked her if anyone had been in Nun's Castle while I was away, and for a minute I wondered if Superintendent Lewis had made a quiet, unofficial check-up. I wouldn't have put it past him. But no, Sylvia admitted to letting in another visitor. "Mr. Lestrange came and had a look round. Just to see if everything was all right while you were away. I thought it was all right." But, of course, anything Ted did was acceptable to her: he employed her husband, and his grandfather had employed her husband's grandfather, and so on. "I'm surprised you knew really. Clever of you. You always were observant."

How had I known? In a moment I realized. The great bunch of house keys which had hung on a hook at one side of the kitchen door had been removed to a hook on the *other* side of the door, thus breaking a tradition of the house. I had noticed this that morning, and unconsciously the implication had been sinking in all this time.

As the sky darkened I gave up hope of the nurse coming. So I was surprised when I heard a timid little tap at the door.

"You didn't think I'd come." She sounded half-nervous, half-aggressive. "But I said I would and I meant to keep my word. You threatened me, didn't you? I can stand up to a threat." But all the same she was trembling with nervousness. "I have nothing to be ashamed of. Some people live up to their ideals. Others ignore them."

She meant me, but I didn't understand why. "You're a sort of parasite, you know, a rather special sort. You live in the past of your country but do not support it."

"I don't know why you dislike me. You *do* dislike me and I believe you dislike my cousin Lynnet."

There was something about Lynnet's name that seemed to silence everybody. It silenced her now. I was beginning to find this unnerving.

Now her color faded. "No. I didn't dislike your cousin. I hardly knew her. She consulted Dr. Timberlake on her marriage to see if she could have a child. She had reason to believe that she could not. He confirmed it."

"Poor Lynnet," I said. "So that's why she ran away."

"She took it badly."

"And her husband? What did he do? Where is he? Who is he?"

Dead silence. "How should I know?"

"Tell me," I said persuasively, "about Lynnet—all about Lynnet."

The wind was banging at the windows and rattling at the lock.

"Oh, there's a Queen in every ride. The trick is to know her."

"Hive, not ride."

"Hide," she said.

She was slurring her words as if she was drunk or drugged. I think now she was merely in a state of profound shock.

She slumped sideways in her chair, her eyes closed. I jumped forward. As far as I could tell she was simply asleep. I let her stay. I had plenty to think about and I might want to ask her more questions when she woke up.

I felt tired myself, but nowhere near sleeping. I went out into the kitchen, leaving her there, and made some coffee and sandwiches. I took my time. Perhaps I hoped she'd have woken up and gone by the time I got back with the food. But she was still there when I walked in. I drank my coffee and ate, and in a little while, it is true, she did stir.

"Drink some coffee." I poured her some in a mug. Her hand looked too unsteady to hold a cup of the fine porcelain I was using.

"Thank you. I'm afraid I dropped off." She was always apologizing to me. "I heard some news that shocked me. You can never tell about people, can you? But I should not ask you."

"But you did." I could not keep a certain astringency from my voice: after all, to fall asleep was strange enough.

"I'm not ill, you know. Just not quite well." Her hands fumbled for a cigarette. "No matches," she said.

I got up. "I'll fetch some," I said. There were usually some matches in the drawer of the hall table. I drew the drawer open. Inside were several boxes of matches, and also something else.

There was a pair of gloves at the bottom of the drawer. My gloves. I picked them up and smelled them. I knew by the scent that they were indeed my gloves and none others. I must have put my gloves away on coming home and forgotten them.

So the gloves which I had given to the police, which were blood-stained, and which so resembled these, were not, after all, my gloves.

I could feel my heart begin to pound. I was working things out fast as my eye traveled from the table to the hall closet, and then back to the table again. I was remembering.

My hand was steady as I lit the cigarette. "I know who killed the doctor," I said.

We stared at each other. I read her eyes. "I think you know, too. And if you don't then I will tell you now: Nesta. She left a pair of blood-stained gloves here and took mine away by mistake. She left them when she came here with the child. She left the child and then took him back."

"Why should she do that?"

"She can explain that to the police," I said. "I expect they will give her every chance."

My visitor stood up. "I've done what I came here to do: to tell you what I could about your cousin Lynnet. I don't see you've proved anything against Nesta. She needn't have worn the gloves herself. Anyone could have done. Your cousin. A man, even."

"You're very unhappy, aren't you?"

"I'm frightened," she said, with desperation. "The past

catches up with you. Look here, you may be in some danger yourself."

"I think Nesta has tried to kill me once," I said. "I rescued myself then. I can look after myself again. And I have friends." I was thinking of David and Ted.

"Lovers, you mean. I know about you and your lovers. You're the Snow Queen in your Maiden's Castle, aren't you? Lucky if ever either one of them gets near you." I opened my mouth to speak, and then let it go. I did not understand what she was saying, but I got the force of the emotion behind it. "Remember this," she went on. "Nesta's child has a father and paternity means a lot to some men."

She meant something pointed by that, I knew. "Lynnet?" I began questioningly.

"Yes, think about what I say *and* think about your cousin. And remember where you live: Nun's Castle."

When the door had banged behind her, I said aloud to the wind-torn air: I never forget that Lynnet and I are coheiresses of Nun's Castle. It seems like our doom.

The wind sucked at the words and drained the volume and sound from them and left them empty syllables, mouthed into the empty room.

I walked slowly to my bed. The castle walls closed round me, dark and claustrophobic.

In defiance I left all the lights burning. The outer doors were bolted. And I put a call through to Joan at the exchange ostensibly to see if I could book a call to New York (with some glee she said several lines were already down in the gale), but really to let her know I was alone in the castle.

In hindsight, perhaps these primitive precautions saved my life.

Sleep was hard to come by, even rest was difficult. Was I really a snow maiden? There was enough truth in the taunt to trouble me. It was true that I had seized a quick excuse to dismiss Ted. Perhaps he would not move out of my life as smoothly as I imagined. Snow Queens are there to be melted, that's the point of them, after all, isn't it, whether they know it or not?

I tossed restlessly, thoughts forming in related clusters in my mind and then breaking up again into isolated points of light. Lynnet was the center of one group of thoughts; Ted Lestrange and his friend Mallard were at the heart of another; Nesta and her child and myself in a third. Several of the characters appeared in more than one group, formed alliances and then drifted off again. Everyone was linked in love or hate.

Sleepily, yet profoundly, my mind was at work. My dreams were full of locks and bolts and deep dark dungeons, the classic symbols of the threatened. I wonder what fearful images primitive man formed in his dreams, but perhaps his dangers were so real and imminent that his sleep was empty.

In the morning the wind had dropped, but it was very cold. A thick hoar frost had covered the scene outside so that it glittered like a hostile Christmas card. There was no love in the countryside that day; the bleak midwinter enmity between nature and the living beasts was nowhere more manifest than in the hard hills, where the soil must be like iron. I put on a thick sweater and trousers and laced my feet into fur-lined boots. Even inside the house the cold crept under the doors and along the floor.

By the time I had dressed I knew what had lain behind

my dream. I walked into the kitchen. The big bunch of house keys had gone. Some time yesterday, after my call to Sylvia Evans, they had been removed in a manner as bold as brass. I found myself repeating the words: bold as brass.

I picked up the white cat, who was following at my heels, and shut her into my bedroom. Then I unbolted the front door and stepped out into the cold world.

I knew that the house was unbreached, and that therefore the keys had been used to unlock one of the outbuildings. After the roaring wind of yesterday the air was still. I was glad of the quiet, as though it would help me check the demonic forces I felt all around me.

And yet this was silly: I had only to ring up the police and ask for help. For any number of reasons they would be bound to rush to me. But when I picked up the telephone the line was dead. Who then were the demons and how did they operate? On whose side were the natural forces playing? It was a question you could ask yourself and ask again.

I tried the door to the bottle dungeon. It was locked. I tried the door leading to the mine tunnel; this too was locked. Only what I had expected. But I knew a trick or two about that lock.

It was an old mortice lock. There was a slackness about its fittings where the old wooden door frame had shrunk and left room for a knife blade to be inserted to push back the bolt of the lock (which was worn and old too) and release the mechanism. I crouched to get a better look. I saw that the door around the lock had been built up with what looked like plastic wood, roughly applied. The filling seemed new.

I understood then that my intruder was someone who had known Nun's Castle as long as I had. Someone I had played with as a child.

This reduced the numbers somewhat, I thought sardonically: Ted, David, Lynnet, and, at a pinch, Sylvia Evans.

The tunnel into which this door led had been dug by the castle defenders to attack their besiegers, who were busily mining in from outside. The mine had its entrance in the wooded hillside close to the now fast-flowing river. It was a large entrance, now fenced in with iron railings. From years ago, I knew that one of these railings could be removed like an old tooth, and that a slim girl could slide through the gap. I went out of the castle to see. The river was slapping at its banks nearby. It was an ugly dank brown, big with the rains and the melted snow. Rain on snow is what every country dweller fears. It swells the rivers with ugly brown water and brings danger of floods. I wondered briefly about the old reservoir and how those puddled walls of mud would hold.

Then I turned back to my problem of squeezing through the railings. I was hardly fatter than when I had last gone through. Only my thick coat would impede my progress. I went back for a flashlight. As I scrambled up the hillside, I stopped for a moment and listened. From a distance came a deep sound, as if the earth itself had said something sharp and anxious. Then silence. I stayed still for a moment, then hurried on.

By now I was motivated by a sort of savage determination to get to the bottom of things. I hardly minded any longer what happened to me in the process. I had been manipulated by another mind long enough. The little cat escaped on this trip to my room and came frisking out round my heels and back to the tunnel with me.

At the mouth of the tunnel I paused for a moment in

dismay. Thistles and brambles were growing across it and a young sapling had twined itself across the face. But it was a slender tree and would not come in my way. I soon saw that my old friend the loose railing was in place and weaker than ever. The rust around it held me up for a minute, but was not in itself enough to stop me. I gave a wrench and the thing came out. In a second I had pushed myself through into the dank cavern beyond. It was more like being in a tomb than I would have conceived possible. Fungi and mosses were creeping up the side of the walls, eating into the once hard-packed earth. As a child I had found it deeply romantic. It reminded me of Byron's Childe Harold and of the heroes of Dumas and Scott, all of whom I had admired. *Now* I thought it a detestable place and shivered with cold and nerves. The cat chattered angrily at some small furry creature peering from a crevice.

I had a strange feeling then. Call it a presentiment or precognition or just a sudden flash of truth. I knew that I was going to see my cousin Lynnet. For better or worse, we were soon going to meet. The questions I would ask her hurried into my mouth. I was as angry as the cat.

I advanced to the end of the mine and stared up to the hole in the roof which led to the smaller tunnel above as it emerged from the castle. The original defenders of the castle probably poured boiling water and stones down on the attackers below. An aged rope dangled there and always had dangled and we shinnied up and down. I suppose I was about twelve the last time I came down that rope. Going up was always harder.

I understood now why I had this strong vision of Lynnet. She was the last person who had played with me in this tunnel and, incredibly, sticking to the rope were two long golden hairs. How bright they seemed to have withstood ten years decay.

With the little cat watching progress from a safe spot I hauled myself up the short rope.

I don't know what I expected, but anyway there was nothing. At some time this upper small tunnel, in which, at this end, a man could just stand upright, had been walled, whitewashed, and fitted with electric light. So I could now view it in its clinical emptiness.

Not quite empty at a second glance, however, for propped against the wall was a spade. There was mossy earth on the spade and blades of grass. The grass was still green.

I stared and cold silent thoughts came bubbling up. I turned away, and moving without conscious thought, I slid down the rope. The cat watched me come down as she had watched me go up.

The flashlight lit the interior for me. I walked to the end of the tunnel, where a small side tunnel had been attempted. The beam moved on. The light caught a glitter of gold. It looked like hair; but how could it be? I felt sick.

I walked forward, following the light. At first I made out no details, only the spill of golden hair. What I saw was a long bundle that could have been anything, except for that hair. But I knew.

"Oh, Lynnet, Lynnet," I said.

We were meeting, after all, but I could not see her face. I would never see it again. She was swathed in layers of polyethylene and only her mane of golden hair showed. She must have been dead soon after she left her suitcase at the railway station. To one side there was what appeared to be a plain, lead coffin. On her breast was a white card on which someone had printed the words:

Lynnet, wife of David Griffith

I could see that, although Lynnet had been dead some time, the preparations for her burial were recent and not yet completed. I had entered the scene halfway through.

At that moment I heard movements in the tunnel above me. My head went up and my muscles stiffened. I cannot describe the emotions of anger and aggression that welled up inside me.

I knew then that I was a hunter. Like a cat I was waiting there, poised to destroy.

I drew back into the shadows. A figure slid down the rope, moving heavily and clumsily, carrying a small lamp. He was heavier than I was and had never been any good with the rope.

He walked forward to stand by the body of his wife. At that moment I had very little doubt that he had killed her.

I was just about to move into the light of his lamp when a voice called through the hole in the roof.

"David? David?" The whisper floated eerily round the runnel.

He didn't answer. The voice tried again.

"Selina, Selina!"

There was something horrible hearing myself called in that way. But neither of us moved.

"Lynnet, Lynnet? Can you answer me, Lynnet?"

This time David did react. With an angry exclamation he spun round and went to stand below the hole. "Stop that," he said.

"What, did you think I could call the dead?" The voice, Nesta's, was mocking.

"Stop it, I say."

"I wish I'd never said anything at all. I wish you'd

never found her. You could have gone on thinking she had killed herself. Or run away. I wish she had, stupid silly girl. I could have killed her many times over. I saw enough of her when I was nursing her brother."

"So you did, so you did. You killed her again every minute you left her here unburied." He sounded near to breaking point, and I remembered his tenderness with small animals. But I hardened my heart. Hunters like me, closing in for the kill, cannot afford sympathy with the prey.

I heard her whisper something which I did not catch, but it was evidently a summons which he obeyed, because he started to climb the rope.

Nesta had been Joe's nurse. Now that I knew this fact, I could understand how well she had known the ways and habits of the house. She had been a part of Joe's life, and Lynnet's life, and my own, too, without my even knowing she was there.

Now that I was hearing her voice without seeing her, I knew that it had been *her* and not Lynnet on the telephone. How could it be Lynnet? Lynnet was dead. No, it had been Nesta, teasing me. Perhaps, at first, she had not even intended to pretend to be my cousin, not until I gave her the cue by asking if she was Lynnet. She had used the calls to torment me at first, then later in order to get me out of Nun's Castle while she went in. As Joe's nurse, Nesta knew Nun's Castle better than anyone. She knew how we lived there and how we could be menaced. Her threats to me had grown more dangerous as David's interest in me had become more obvious, until in the end she wanted me dead. They made a strange pair and their relationship puzzled me. There was sex in it and anger, I could detect both in their voices, but there was something else as well. Together they seemed to make up some double-headed monster. Nesta had killed Lynnet because she was jealous, but I felt that there must have been another reason. David's reaction to his wife's murder was ambiguous. Nesta had a power over David that went beyond love. The tie that bound them together was not to be broken even by murder.

I backed away, but not in fear. I was full of anger. I would go back through the tunnel, up the hill and meet them face to face. They were looking for me. *I* was looking for them.

All the time I had been listening to David and Nesta, I had been conscious of another sound in the background. A dull, swift, muted roar.

Now I knew what it was. As I came toward the mouth of the tunnel water, getting deeper every minute, was swirling round my feet.

The reservoir must have burst its banks, and the river was in flood. The snow, the rain upon the snow, then this bitter frost had strained the patched and broken reservoir beyond its strength. I could imagine the frost cracking the walls, first in a narrow hair-line split, and soon in a quickly widening gap through which the dammed-up water would pour. I knew now what had caused the noise I heard earlier: it must have been the first moment when the earth moved.

Outside the barred entrance to the tunnel I could see the brown, rushing water. It was already deep enough for me to find no easy foothold when I pushed through the bars again. There would be a moment or two of real danger before I could scramble up to the dry ground of the hill. The water was moving strongly too, and I thought of the Devil's

Sink in mid-river and wondered how far its power could now reach and whether its unseen mouth was already sucking all toward it.

At that moment I had a choice: I could climb the rope to face David and Nesta, and whatever fate they might choose to hand out to me, or I could trust myself to the river.

Of the two dangers I preferred the river. I meant to see David and Nesta face to face, but it should be in my own way and as I chose.

The water was high above my ankles as I waded toward the tunnel entrance. To my dismay I saw that the force of the water had brought a young tree down and smashed it across my exit. It looked as though it was wedged firmly in the hole I hoped to squeeze through. I took a deep breath and pushed. The wood moved; but not sufficiently. A second, and a third push produced even less effect. I might even be jamming it in position more strongly.

All the time the water was rising. I looked back up the tunnel and saw the water was advancing in it. I repressed all thoughts of her who lay there, dead, where the waters might cover her.

I could see that the tree trunk had somehow got stuck at the bottom, and that if I could dislodge it there then the rest would follow easily. I bent down, crouching in the water, and felt with my hand. I made my fingers probe and push, seeking for a weak spot. Leaves and twigs were hindering my efforts; I pulled them away, but others seemed to come in their place at once. It seemed hopeless. I reached up and shook the railings on either side of the tree. I turned my shoulder to its wood and pushed. I felt it give. I shoved harder. It moved. One last thrust and slowly, slowly, it sank backwards. I pushed myself through the gap. It seemed harder getting out than getting in. I felt as though I must have swollen. There was one horrible claustrophobic moment with the water swirling round my legs and my feet slipping all ways and my chest tightly compressed between the bars, when I felt as though I would suffocate. Then I was through, and out the other side.

It was then I remembered the white cat.

She was still inside, somewhere. I knew I could not leave her to drown.

I pushed myself back through the gap. I moved forward cautiously, playing the beam of the flashlight this way and that. I couldn't see her. I remember calling: "Puss, puss," softly. I had to think of the pair above. With increasing anxiety I looked for the cat, but she seemed to be gone. Then I caught the green flash of her eyes in the dark. She was crouched silently on a shelf of stone about a foot long and above my head. Even in my mood as it was then, I saluted a natural survivor. All the same, I could not leave her. I plucked her down and holding her tightly against me, turned again. She hung on with all twenty efficient claws. We stared at each other silently, before the two of us squeezed through the bars, with me now knee-deep. I had the knack now and got us through easily. Outside I caught my breath. I could see now that the river was running fast and deep and menacingly. I stepped out boldly, and at once found that I was nearly out of my depth. The ground sloped sharply here, and I had misjudged my step. I floundered, water dashing into my face. The cat crawled up toward my shoulder, scratching my throat as she went. There was nothing for it, turning sideways to keep the cat above the water, I struck out, swimming. Some water got up my nose and down my throat. It tasted vegetable and sour. I coughed, instinctively trying to clear away the taste. Almost at once, I felt the pull of the current. The distance was so small, and yet I seemed to draw no closer. Instead I felt the suck of the water toward the middle of the river. It was strong and urgent. It was also piercingly cold. My labored progress brought me close to a tree. Before the river rose this tree had been a graceful object, shaped by the prevailing winds. Now it was half under water. But I grabbed it, dragged myself toward it and hung on. Behind me stretched the turbulent river, in front rose the slope leading up to Nun's Castle. On the other side of the tree a long slender branch leaned forward to the upper slope. If I could make my way to it I should be safe, and the cat with me. All the time I had been conscious of her light weight and anxious breathing, but she had been perfectly quiet.

I started to edge round the tree, holding on with one hand. I felt something bump against me. I turned and, to my surprise, found myself looking into the long innocent face of a sheep. Only, being one of David's special sheep, its face was not so innocent, but had a knowing look. The animal was paddling itself with apparent aimlessness, but I saw its eyes flick towards the sloping grass verge ahead. Without conscious thought I reached out and grabbed its thick coat, more hair than wool. It gave me a reproachful glance over its shoulder but did not stop its slow paddle. In a minute it gave a heave, scrabbled with its front legs and scrambled up on to the grass.

Sheep, girl and cat, we had all three landed.

Still hugging the cat, I scrambled up the hill to Nun's Castle. Behind us the sheep immediately began to nibble the grass. But the cat and I were hunters; each had other hungers to feed.

They were still talking in the upper tunnel when I crept to the door, now open. I heard my own name: Selina. "Yes, wait for Selina," I thought. "Name her, talk about her, but above all wait to see what she will do."

"Let's put her at the bottom of her own dungeon and leave her there," said Nesta.

"If you touch one hair of Selina's head I promise I will kill you." But David sounded weary rather than angry. "You killed her two cousins, leave it at that. Won't that do?"

"I didn't kill Joe. He killed himself," she said. "He nearly killed *me*. God, the strength he had in those arms. He was *savage* when he heard you had married Lynnet. He kept on and on at me till he got it out. I wouldn't have told him otherwise, David."

"Especially as she was dead already," he said savagely.

"She came to me, David, almost asking to be killed. She came to me as a nurse. She knew I was a nurse. She told me Timberlake had told her she could never have a child. She knew I had your child, she wanted to adopt him. And then, when she was there, she saw . . ." Her voice for the first time hesitated.

"She saw the old man, I suppose, poor kid," said David.

"Yes. It was a shock to her, David. She was so hysterical I knew she had to go. She would have told *everything*."

He muttered something that I couldn't hear.

"No, let her stay secretly buried. All great leaders have their secrets; they all come to power over other people's dead bodies."

She was not mad, but she was a fanatic, the sort of girl who would throw bombs, machine-gun her enemies, create a guerrilla group of destroyers.

I had pictured David and Nesta as one being with two heads. I saw now that what united them so thoroughly was a common madness, stronger than sex, stronger than any love. Together they were breeding revolution; but it was a backward looking, nostalgic revolution, turning its gaze toward a golden dream of a past which had never existed. I blamed Nesta most: David was the dreamer, but Nesta was the true revolutionary.

I moved quietly forward to where I could see David.

He was standing looking at her, his face in profile, his hands in his pockets. I saw him for what he was, a weak dreamer, lost in a romantic mist. Imaginatively tracing his descent down through the centuries from a great Prince, forgetting the generations of quiet farmers that lay between, and seeing himself as the Prince reborn. There were worlds between him and Nesta. And Selina and Lynnet, silly girls, had been the Princesses in the Castle, the unlucky brides whose dowry was Nun's Castle, the site sacred to David's hero. He was all corrupted by false dreams of the past. It would be wrong to say I understood all this at this one moment of crisis, but comprehension had been slowly forming within me ever since my visit to the Davies farm.

I heard my name again. Selina. Selina. I moved forward to the door. "What about Selina, David?" I said.

I knew I was taking my life in my hands. The violence in Nesta, and the hate, and the willingness to kill were so strong.

"Am I to go in the bottle dungeon, Nesta?" I said

turning to her. "I knew the nurse from the Clinic would go straight back and tell you I suspected you. You could say I sent her to you. You had just told her about Lynnet, hadn't you? She was in a state of shock still when she came to see me." I deliberately made my voice cold and contemptuous. It was hard to remain in control and not be furiously angry.

She stared at me silently; for the moment discomposed. Then she took a deliberate step sideways and I saw what I had not seen before, a shotgun, leaning against the wall. She seized it, and brought its twin barrels level with my breast.

"It won't be necessary to use the dungeon," she said. "We could bury you here with your cousin."

I looked like a victim, but I was really a predator. Nesta ought to fear me.

"You've had one shot at polishing me off," I reminded her, "when it became clear David would try to marry *me*. You're a classic case, really. But poison should be your weapon and not a gun."

I didn't look at David. I felt so sorry for him, so terribly sorry when I remembered our youth together. I had loved him a little, and trusted him, and, in a way, honored him. So I didn't dare look. Oh, I was sorry for him, sorry. The past and the present were terribly alive together in this narrow space. There wasn't room for it all.

David said something low and quick of which I heard only one word "save."

"There's nothing to save, David," I said. "It's all lost. Ted Lestrange has a Special Branch policeman called Mallard after you."

I never took my eyes off Nesta as she slipped off the safety catch of the gun. "No one knows I'm here talking to you, Nesta," I said. "I'm anonymous, darling. Go on, do it."

She moistened her lips. I could see her knuckles whiten as she began slowly to squeeze the gun's trigger. David gave a groan and made a sudden grab at her arm. The gun jerked and moved direction, and went off. The shot hit David full in the chest, slightly above the heart, but the effect was mortal. I saw him twist and fall. Nesta stood there looking dazed, ridiculous and damned. Then she sank to her knees and began to cry.

The roar of the explosion had reverberated round the narrow chamber, filling my ears with noise. I heard the report of the second shot as I ran toward the house.

I went to the telephone in the sunlit hall. Miraculously, the line was open and working. Ted answered straight away, almost as if he had been expecting a call.

"Come and get me," I said, nothing more, and put down the telephone, cutting off Joan's deep and interested breathing. The news that our marriage was on again would be round the valley in no time at all.

While I was waiting for him I went to the great window and stared out. The clouds had parted and a gleam of pale sunlight had appeared.

I opened the window and leaned out. Below me, I could hear the voice of the river as it rushed along its course. It was a strange noise to hear in Catt's Tower where usually only the birds and the sheep interrupted the silence. Nature, which looks so tranquil and peaceful here in the hills, had just given me a quick touch of her other side.

Instead of standing here, I might now have been dead, my body carried along by the brown and surging water until it was twisting endlessly round and round in the Devil's Sink. Or I might have been shot dead and left to lie with Lynnet.

I moved from the window and sat down in a chair, my legs weak. The energy and determination which had carried me through the encounter with Nesta and David were spent. I felt sick and frightened, as I had not felt while the battle (for it *had* been a battle) had lasted. I was overjoyed to see Ted when he arrived. Not even the floods had stopped him from getting to me.

The waters rose no higher, but for some hours still lay on the land, neither rising nor falling. Sylvia Evans, coming in later that day to see me, told me, in a hushed whisper, that the water was shining in the sunlight like a shield. "Like a silver shield," she said, with unexpected poetry.

A few low-lying houses were inundated with water, and some sheep and cows had to be rescued, but the total damage was surprisingly little. A sheet of water spread itself out over the countryside and then gradually retreated.

During this period when, I suppose, I was still in a state of shock, I saw both Superintendent Lewis and the policeman Mallard from the Special Branch. I remember only snatches of our conversations together, but I recall enough to know that they told me Nesta and David had both been involved in a serious plot. Mallard pulled a long face and would not be explicit about details, but Ted told me afterward that a good many arrests, up and down the country, could be expected. Both policemen were gentle and polite toward me. Forensic evidence bore out my story of how David and Nesta had died. David had been killed by a shot from Nesta's gun. Nesta had shot herself; her hand still clutched the gun.

Some of the last moments of my cousin Joe's life were clearer to me now. Joe was perceptive, as Ted had remarked. He was in such close contact with Nesta that he must have begun to guess the secret life she was creating. The alert outsider, he had been able to observe Nesta, David and Lady Dorothy creating their fantasies. He had never liked David. I could imagine his rage when he discovered Lynnet was married to David. No wonder Lynnet had tried to run away. Too proud and angry to talk about it properly, Joe had dropped only puzzling hints to Ted, whom he should have trusted. There had been so much anger as well as love in Joe's feeling for me and his sister.

But between Nesta and Joe there must have erupted a fierce, flaring quarrel. I could only guess which of these violent creatures had started it. I could imagine Joe gripping at Nesta with his powerful hands, dragging her toward him and then, perhaps, throwing her away from him as I had seen him throw a glass. Nesta would never have taken the attack easily. She was stronger and bigger built than Lynnet and much more physically aggressive. She would have fought back. I remembered that torn fingernail and wondered what other signs of a struggle I would have seen on Joe's hands if I had examined them. But his heart had taken the main toll, and he had died, as much a victim of his own anger as Nesta's.

I was beginning to see what part everyone had played. But there was one question still unanswered. Nesta and David had been poor, but to fulfill their plans they would have needed money. Financial aid must have been forthcoming from somewhere. I thought it might have come from Lady Dorothy, and, to a lesser extent from Dr. Timberlake. I wondered how well the doctor and Nesta, a nurse, after all, had known each other. She was an attractive, magnetic figure and she might very well have involved him in a relationship which gave her a hold over him. I did let myself wonder if there might not have been a hint of blackmail between them. Dr. Timberlake was a genuinely tragic figure. He was a man worth sparing but Nesta had not spared him. Perhaps he had threatened to tell all that he knew about Lynnet to me or to the police. He had given some indication of doing this. And once a real police investigation about Lynnet started who could tell what might come out? Nesta had been the woman who had telephoned him and then lured him to his death. If lured was the word; perhaps he went willingly, tired of it all. He had looked to me a man at the end of his tether. Deadly, deadly Nesta, destroying all she touched.

I was visited by Lady Dorothy. She was humble and knew her place. She had behaved unwisely and now she knew it. Given time, she would soon bounce back and be the dominating figure we knew, but at the moment she wanted reassurance. I was silent about one episode, because I guessed she would be reluctant to speak. It was clear to me that she had been the person who ordered the baby basket from New York for Nesta's baby. It was the sort of generous impulse that was characteristic of her, giving a lot of trouble to the cousin in America who, no doubt, did the actual ordering for her, and bestowing most of the pleasure on Dorothy herself. I knew why she had chosen the basket too. She had been attracted by the decorative motif of red lions. Red lions were the heraldic symbol of the old Welsh princes from whom, it amused Lady Dorothy to imagine, the child could claim descent through his father. It was a game with her, but deadly serious to Nesta. I now had a new light on the minor mystery of the heraldry of the wall-painting in the chapel. The mysterious donor and founder was thus made out to be a lady of royal blood, probably, in view of the English royal arms also present, the daughter of Llywellyn, last native Prince of Wales. It was an interesting suggestion and I wondered how much evidence could be made out for it. The innocent antiquarianism displayed in this had been a side of Lady Dorothy which Nesta had exploited for her own ends. David's nationalism was romantic and unworldly; he had identified himself with a long dead Prince he claimed as his ancestor. He was the living representative of a man long dead. Nun's Castle was a sacred site, and Lynnet and Selina were the princesses of the fairy tower, one of whom he must marry. So from a murder seven centuries ago sprang a new chain of violence. On the telephone I spoke to the County Archivist. He had resurrected the document I wanted, and he thought it would be complete enough for fingerprints. When I heard this I spoke to Phoebe.

"*You* sent me a photocopy of the marriage certificate, Phoebe, didn't you?"

She nodded. "I wanted you to know about Lynnet."

"But, Phoebe—why put *my* name there?"

She hesitated. "I guessed, and questioned Lynnet about it; she asked me to say nothing. I promised most faithfully I would not. So I didn't. But I wanted you to investigate. And I knew *you*. I knew you'd go back to the original document." She smiled faintly. She didn't apologize. It had not been her fault I was in an imaginative sensitive state when I received her strange missive.

"Did you know about the fire in the Church of St. Kenelm, Phoebe?" I asked.

"Yes, of course. You're not accusing me of starting it, I hope?" She laughed dryly. "I'm no arsonist."

"Is it known how the fire happened then?"

"If you ever looked at the local papers you'd know that the police found some fingerprints on a can of paraffin and this led them to a lad who had started a fire in another church a year ago. He was on probation."

"And now he's getting medical treatment, I suppose," I said sceptically.

"That's right."

"Well, I hope it cures him."

"Oh, he'll be cured of setting fires, I have no doubt. Some other malady will take its place, though. Still, he certainly gives you your answer about the fire. No doubt about it."

There's an answer to everything, I thought, if you can only find it. Inside me I was weeping. Ted knew and old Lizzie guessed, but perhaps no one else.

Ted was very gentle to me and kind. He made no reference to our quarrel and seemed willing to go on as if it had never happened. I knew I owed him some amends, and was casting round for the way to do it gracefully, when he made it unnecessary. We had to talk business together because he was an executor of Joe's will. The lawyer from Hereford drove over and talked solemnly to me in Ted's presence about my responsibilities as a landowner. When he had finished he looked at Ted and waited. Ted said: "Selina, I have suggested a plan for Nun's Castle and the land that goes with it." He stressed the words "and the land that goes with it" very slightly. "I have set aside a sum of my own money and propose to use it to endow Nun's Castle as a national monument. We can put it in good order, do whatever work is necessary. I hope you will superintend it yourself, it's the sort of thing you would do well, and then it can be open to the public. But the property is yours; it is for you to say yes, or no."

Mr. Bohun, the lawyer, looked at me over his spectacles and said: "You have to remind yourself, Miss Brewse, that this land of yours has some valuable mining rights. We have had more than one offer to buy."

"I don't want to exploit them," I said. I turned gratefully to Ted. "Nun's Castle is my inheritance, but its history belongs to the whole country. I accept your offer."

"I believe Lady Dorothy might let us have the chapel too," he said. "She's rather gone off her historical studies at the moment." He grinned, and I smiled back. So many diverse strands of my life came together at that healing moment. I knew then that with Ted I could combine my love of learning, my feeling for the past, my pleasure in being a woman, a life as a whole person.

We were married quietly just after Christmas. When we returned from our short wedding trip we went up to the Davies's farm to collect the child whom we were to adopt. Old Lizzie had been up there looking after him for the last few weeks. We took him home together, Ted's home and mine now, not Nun's Castle. The white cat was already in residence.

We left one last inhabitant of the farm who very soon, in his turn, would be moved away. He came to stand in the door and watch us depart.

Tall, gaunt, a mane of hair waving over his collar, a figure from the past. I knew who he was now: Joe and Lynnet's father, the spellbinder, the man with the golden voice. Dreams and visions shattered, he had crept secretly back to Davies's Farm, the home of one of his greatest supporters.

He stood there now, looking at us, the source of much of the tragedy that had spilled out on his family. His gaze flickered to me, unknowing. No saint, still less a martyr or a hero, just a crazed witless old fellow, his mind quite gone.

I picked up the child and got into the car. The future was there waiting and what we made of it was up to us.